D0459866

COUNT ME IN

SARA LEACH

ORCA BOOK PUBLISHERS

Library and Archives Canada Cataloguing in Publication

Leach, Sara, 1971-
Count me in / Sara Leach.

Issued also in electronic format.
ISBN 978-1-55469-404-4

I. Title.
PS8623.E253C69 2011   JC813'.6   C2011-903334-8

First published in the United States, 2011
Library of Congress Control Number: 2011929245

Summary: In order to survive on a hiking trip to a remote BC lake, Tabitha must face
danger, adversity and her cousin Ashley's hatred.

FSC
MIX
Paper from
responsible sources
www.fsc.org
FSC® C016245

*Orca Book Publishers is dedicated to preserving the environment and has printed
this book on paper certified by the Forest Stewardship Council®.*

Orca Book Publishers gratefully acknowledges the support for its publishing
programs provided by the following agencies: the Government of Canada through the
Canada Book Fund and the Canada Council for the Arts, and the Province of British
Columbia through the BC Arts Council and the Book Publishing Tax Credit.

Cover design by Teresa Bubela
Cover images by Getty Images and Dreamstime.com
Author photo by Bob Brett

ORCA BOOK PUBLISHERS
PO Box 5626, STN. B
VICTORIA, BC CANADA
V8R 6S4

ORCA BOOK PUBLISHERS
PO Box 468
CUSTER, WA USA
98240-0468

www.orcabook.com
Printed and bound in Canada.

14 13 12 11 • 4 3 2 1

To Jane

CHAPTER ONE

Tabitha dropped her pack and collapsed onto the nearest boulder. As she wiped the sweat from her face, her cousins slipped off their hiking boots and ran, fully clothed, into the lake.

"Last one in burns the toilet paper!" Cedar shouted as he dove into the water.

Tabitha frowned. What did that mean? It was one more example of how her cousins were a club of two—a club to which she'd never belong.

She pulled off her right boot and sock and examined a large red spot on her heel. Her toes were wrinkled from being squished in her boot during the long hike. Maybe a swim in the lake would be refreshing. If only the water didn't look so cold.

Lake Lovely Water, the goal of their grueling hike, stretched before her. She had to admit it did look, well, lovely. Five snow-spotted peaks were reflected in the turquoise water. The dark green trees on their lower flanks seemed to grow directly from the lake. Her eyes followed the ridgeline as she counted the smaller bumps between each peak. Five. Eight. Thirteen. Her kind of numbers. She'd learned about the Fibonacci string at a summer math camp and liked the idea that it went on forever, and that the numbers could be found in nature, like on sunflowers and tree branches. She closed her eyes and recited the first part of the string to herself: 1, 1, 2, 3, 5, 8, 13, 21. She relaxed a little with the familiar comfort of counting. Maybe this place wasn't so bad.

The only sign of civilization was the brightly painted yellow and red hut on the shore to her right. Aunt Tess was climbing the steps beside Max, Uncle Bruce's golden retriever. Tabitha shook her head. Not her uncle's dog, not anymore. It had been over a year, but she still sometimes forgot that he was dead.

Ashley swooshed her arm through the water. "Are you coming in, or what?"

Tabitha kicked off her other boot and pulled her knees to her chest. She didn't like swimming in her clothes. They swished around her body like slippery eels.

She didn't like skinny-dipping either. Not that she had anything to hide. But Cedar was a boy, an older boy, even if he was her cousin.

She slid a foot off the rock. "How cold is it?"

"It's great!" Cedar shouted. He flicked his ponytail, spraying drops through the air like a dog shaking. Everything he did was loud. Loud and big.

Tabitha took a tentative step onto the rocks. They jabbed at her tender feet. As she reached the shore, cold gray mud oozed through her toes. She stopped.

"Come on," Cedar said. "If you wait too long, you'll cool off."

Everything was easy for her cousins. They were strong and fast, like mountain lions. They had practically run up the trail. Tabitha felt awkward and slow— all elbows and knees, like a baby deer. Her mom told her that she needed time to grow into her body. Right. She'd probably be a skinny, clumsy eighty-year-old bumping down the hallways of an old-age home.

Cedar and Ashley even had cool names. Cedar was named after the yellow cedar trees that grew all over the mountains; Ashley was named after the graceful mountain ash. Tabitha was named after her grandmother. Yippee.

Tabitha brushed the dirt off her legs. Time to stop feeling sorry for herself. Not everything was easy for Ashley and Cedar. Their dad was dead, after all.

"Come on!" Cedar called. "Aren't you hot after the hike?"

She *was* hot. And sweaty. And sticky. She'd been hiking all day. They had started from her cousins' home in Squamish before the sun rose that morning, driving along a bumpy road to the Squamish River. The half-hour ride was quiet. Cedar appeared to be asleep, while Ashley stared out the window with a deep crease between her brows. Maybe everyone was tired, or maybe they were thinking about what lay ahead. Aunt Tess hardly said anything the entire ride. Every once in a while, she'd pat the bag beside her. Tabitha shuddered. It gave her the heebie-jeebies that they were riding in the same truck as Uncle Bruce's ashes.

When they had arrived at the river, Ashley and Cedar perked up, as though they could relax now that the real journey had begun. They sprang into action, unloading the canoe from the roof of the truck and laying the packs in the bottom of it.

Aunt Tess, Ashley and Cedar had paddled across the river while Tabitha cowered in the middle of the canoe with Max and the backpacks, wishing there was another way to get to the trailhead. Blue water swirled around them. Tabitha was sure it would tip the canoe and drown them at any moment. Her cousins seemed unconcerned, splashing each other with their paddles and pointing to birds flying overhead. Tabitha didn't care about eagles. She closed her eyes, wrapped her arms around Max's chubby body and cursed her parents for making her come on the trip. Did they think a near-death experience would solve her problems at school?

Once they had reached the other side and secured the canoe, the really hard part started. After fifteen minutes of hiking straight up, sweat was pouring down Tabitha's face. When she wiped it away, her hair stuck to her cheek. She wished she had short hair like Ashley, who looked as if she'd just hopped out of the shower. Or that she'd brought an elastic to hold her hair back, the way Cedar did. It didn't seem fair that she and Cedar both had straight brown hair, but his looked shiny and thick, while hers hung limply around her face. Tabitha's mom and Aunt Tess were sisters, but obviously Cedar and Ashley had gotten all the good genes.

The "trail" was a narrow path through thick forest. Sometimes they didn't even follow a path but looked for pieces of fluorescent orange flagging tape hanging high in the tree branches. What if a bird ripped off a piece of tape to help make its nest, or someone tied the tape to the wrong trees? They could have been lost for days.

Her aunt led the way at a stiff pace. After half an hour, Tabitha was dying for a break. No one even noticed her panting at the back.

"Remember the time Dad carried the watermelon all the way up the trail and didn't tell us?" Cedar said.

Aunt Tess turned around and smiled. "He kept complaining about his heavy pack."

"No," Ashley said. "He never complained. He just pulled out the watermelon when we got to the lake."

Cedar squinted at Ashley. "He did too complain. He whined the whole way up. What are you talking about?"

Aunt Tess flashed a warning look at Cedar. "Maybe we remember it wrong." She turned and marched up the hill even faster than before.

Finally, after an hour, they stopped for a water break. As Tabitha sank to the ground and gulped from her water bottle, heat-seeking missiles began attacking her. She swatted them with her hands.

"Aunt Tess, is there any mosquito repellent?" she asked.

"No," her aunt replied. "We don't use it. Studies have linked it to cancer. It's better to keep moving. And you're old enough now to call me plain old Tess."

By the third stop, Tabitha's water was almost gone. The creeks they'd passed were so dry only a trickle of mud ran down them. Even Tess, whom Tabitha had seen cut the mold off bread before using the rest for sandwiches, didn't want to drink it. She'd had to hike into the bush to find fresh water. She had come back holding a full bottle of clear water.

"I finally found a creek that was moving." She had popped in an iodine tablet and shaken the bottle. "It'll be ready in half an hour."

At least there was plenty to drink now that they were at Lovely Water. Tabitha swatted a mosquito. If she went in the lake, she'd get away from the bugs. She stepped in the water up to her knees and gasped. "It's freezing!"

"Duh!" Ashley said. "It's a glacial lake. What did you expect?"

Tabitha's shoulders tensed. How was she supposed to know? Ashley and Cedar had been on millions of hikes together. This was her first. What was a glacial lake anyway? She wouldn't dare admit to Ashley that she didn't know.

Cedar must have read her mind. He pointed to the snow on top of the mountains. "Those are glaciers. The snow stays there all summer long. But some of it melts and flows into the lake."

Ashley leaned into the water and grabbed a handful of the gray mud. "This stuff is silt. It's the dirt that flows into the lake with the glacier. It's really slimy, see?" She threw it at Tabitha.

Tabitha jerked back, but the mud splattered across her shirt. "Hey!"

Tears pricked her eyes. Ashley was thirteen, but sometimes she acted like a seven-year-old. Ashley always made a big deal about the fact that she was six months older than Tabitha. Now that she had boobs and Tabitha didn't, she was ten times worse than she'd been before. Tabitha would not let Ashley see her cry. She set her shoulders and ran into the water, right up to her waist.

Her breath caught in her throat. Her legs went numb. She turned to run back to shore, but Cedar grabbed her and dragged her into the water.

"You're wet now. You might as well go all the way in."

"Cut it out!" Tabitha kicked and squirmed, but Cedar was too strong.

She struggled to get away from his grasp. "Let go!"

Finally he did, and she dropped to the bottom of the lake. It was so cold that she gasped again and inhaled a mouthful of water. Pushing herself to the surface, she waded, choking and spluttering, to shore.

She pushed silty hair out of her eyes. Why did they always have to be so mean?

"I wasn't trying to hurt you," Cedar said. "I thought it'd be easier if you went in all at once."

"It wasn't." Tabitha threw on her boots, leaving them untied, and stormed off toward the hut.

CHAPTER TWO

As Tabitha approached the hut, Max bounded off the steps to greet her. He ran in circles around her legs, licking the water off her calves.

"Stop! That tickles." She laughed. So far, he was the best part of the trip. The whole way up the trail, he'd circled between her and the cousins, keeping her company and letting her know she was part of the group. She hugged him, not caring that his long blond hair stuck to her wet skin.

She remembered the first time she'd met Max, eight years ago, when she was four. It had been love at first sight. He was six weeks old, a puffy yellow bundle that had tumbled into her lap when she visited her cousins while they were living in Vancouver.

He licked her face and burrowed into her neck. She'd been begging her parents for a dog, but her dad was allergic to them. Instead, they'd taken her to see Uncle Bruce's new puppy. For the next two months she'd visited her cousins as often as possible, until Tess was finished the courses she was taking at the university and they moved back to Squamish.

Now Max was just as fluffy, but a whole lot bigger. He ran up the steps to the hut. Tabitha pushed open the heavy wooden door and stepped into the dark interior. She stood and blinked for a moment as her eyes adjusted to the light.

Her aunt was bustling around the hut, unpacking her backpack. She'd put on a fleece in the cool air of the hut and hung up her sunhat on a hook by the door. Her long gray hair hung in a ponytail down her back.

"Fall in the lake?" Tess asked.

If Tabitha told her what happened, Tess would say something to Ashley and Cedar, and they'd call her a snitch all weekend. "I went for a swim," she said.

Tess raised her eyebrows. "You're dripping all over the floor. Better get those clothes off and hang them to dry in the sun. You'll need them for our hike tomorrow."

Tabitha nodded. More hiking. She couldn't wait.

"Sleeping quarters are upstairs." Her aunt pointed to a ladder. "You get first choice of bunks."

Hefting her pack onto her back, Tabitha climbed the ladder to the sleeping loft. According to Tess, they had packed light, since the hut was supplied with pots, pans, dishes and foamies for sleeping. But her pack hadn't felt light on the miserable hike up the mountain, and it didn't feel light now. If she'd had to carry anything else, she never would have made it.

The sleeping loft had five bunks, plus room on the floor for more people to sleep. After stripping off her clothes and putting on fleece pants, a dry shirt and a sweater, she felt better. She grabbed a foamie from the floor and put it on a bottom bunk in the corner. Hopefully Ashley and Cedar would choose the bunks by the window, as far away from her as possible.

Her cousins clomped into the hut below her. Tabitha swung down the ladder and moved aside for them to climb up.

"What's for dinner?" she asked.

Tess lit the campstove. "Curried chickpeas with carrots and millet."

Tabitha tried not to gag. "Great."

Tess dumped carrots into a pot and added some water. "I hope you're hungry, because I'm making lots."

Tabitha was starving. But hungry enough to eat chickpeas and millet? Not that it looked like there was any choice.

"How come you use the campstove when there's a woodstove over there?" she asked.

Her aunt stirred the pot. "The woodstove is good for keeping us warm and making tea, but this campstove is much faster for cooking food. Watch this for me while I get some wood, will you? You three need to warm up after your swim."

Tabitha nodded. She watched, hoping nothing would boil over or burn. She had no idea how to turn the stove down. Even if she did, there was no way she'd put her hands near the blue flame hissing out of it.

A minute later, Tess reappeared at the door just as Cedar and Ashley came downstairs. She was hauling a canvas log carrier full of wood. "Tabitha, come give me a hand with this."

Tabitha ran over and grabbed the handles of the canvas. They slipped out of her hands and dropped to the floor. "Sorry," she said. "I didn't know it would be so heavy."

"Of course it's heavy." Cedar scooped the carrier up off the floor as Tabitha tried to stuff the fallen wood back in. "It's full of wood."

She looked away. "I guess I wasn't thinking. Sorry."

Cedar swung the bag as if it were as light as a purse and dropped the wood into a basket beside the stove. "Should I light a fire?"

"Yes, please," said Tess.

Cedar started laying the newspaper and small sticks into the woodstove. Tabitha backed toward the table and bumped into Ashley.

"Hey, watch where you're going," Ashley said.

"Sorry." Tabitha looked around the room, feeling useless. "Anything else I can do, Tess?"

"You could get out the bowls and cutlery."

She'd do anything to get out of the way of Cedar and Ashley. Their bodies felt too big for the cabin. There was no room for her. She edged past the table and opened a few cupboards until she found what she needed. Swinging around to bring them to the table, she banged her hip on the corner of the counter. She jumped back and collided with her aunt.

Startled, Tabitha lurched forward to regain her balance and dropped her load of bowls. They clattered across the floor.

Ashley and Cedar hovered over her as she scrambled to pick up the bowls. "Hope you didn't break anything," Ashley said. "Otherwise you'll have to eat out of Max's dish for the weekend."

Tabitha stayed on her knees after she'd picked up the bowls, fighting back the tears. Why did Ashley always have to pick on her? Finally she stood up. "Nothing broke. They're made of some kind of plastic."

Tess took the bowls from her. "We've had dishes like this at home for years. When Ashley was a baby, she threw them on the floor all the time."

Ashley scowled and marched to the table, plopping onto a bench. Cedar grinned. "We keep trying to break the ones at home 'cause they're so ugly and Mom won't buy new ones until they're all gone, but nothing works."

Tabitha smiled. Cedar wasn't so bad sometimes.

Tess turned off the campstove and lit three candles on the table. Max's gentle panting filled the silence after the hissing of the gas stopped. "Dinner's ready," Tess said. "Let's eat."

Tabitha sat on the bench at the opposite end of the table from Ashley, grateful to be out of everyone's way. Ashley served the chickpeas and millet, passing her an extra large serving. Tabitha eyed it. Had Ashley guessed how she felt about the food and done it on purpose? She took a bite. The flavor wasn't too bad, except for the spiciness, but the texture was awful. Mushy chickpeas mixed with gooey balls of millet. She choked down another bite.

Halfway through the bowl, she gave up. She was still hungry, but she couldn't face another chickpea. Using her spoon, she grouped the remaining chickpeas into piles, hoping that no one would notice that she wasn't eating. 1, 1, 2, 3, 5, 8, 13. There wasn't enough room in her bowl for a group of 21.

"What're you doing?" Ashley asked.

Tabitha shrugged and mushed all the chickpeas together.

"Don't you like the food my mom made?" Ashley asked, her voice loud and snarky.

"I'm just full."

Ashley sneered. "Well, you'd better finish eating 'cause you can't throw it out. We have to pack out what we pack in, and I'm not carrying your leftovers home."

"That's enough, Ashley," Tess said.

Cedar reached for Tabitha's bowl. "I'll eat it."

Tabitha smiled in relief and passed Cedar her bowl.

"I'd like to propose a toast," Tess said. She lifted her mug of water. "To Dad. I'm sure he's watching us now, wishing he were here."

Ashley and Cedar froze, then lifted their cups to clink with Tess's. Tabitha raised hers in the air, not quite touching the others.

"To Dad," they whispered.

"To Uncle Bruce," Tabitha said. She followed Tess's gaze to the kitchen, where the box with the ashes sat on the top shelf of the open cabinet beside the matches and a tin of tea.

"It's strange being here without him, isn't it?" Tess said.

Cedar nodded. His eyes glistened in the candlelight.

Tabitha tried to shrink into the bench. Uncle Bruce had died in a mountaineering accident fifteen months earlier. This was the first time the family had been on their annual Thanksgiving hike to Lake Lovely Water since his death.

The fire crackled in the woodstove, and Tess jumped up, breaking the tension at the table. She opened the black door and added another log. "Good job on the fire, Cedar. Dad couldn't have done any better."

Cedar smiled. "Thanks."

Ashley scowled and muttered into her bowl.

"What?" Cedar said.

"I said, *Yes, he would have.*"

"Would have what?" asked Tess.

"Would have made a better fire."

"I was complimenting Cedar," Tess said. "That doesn't mean I was saying bad things about your father."

Cedar scooped up the last of Tabitha's chickpeas. "Forget it."

"How about some dessert?" Tess held a squished bag of one-bite brownies over the table.

"Sounds good," said Cedar, grabbing four. Tabitha watched in amazement as he popped them into his mouth one after another. If she did that, she'd throw up.

Cedar was still chewing his brownies when Tess put on her boots and walked out of the hut. She came back a few minutes later carrying a metal bucket. Ashley and Cedar groaned.

"Couldn't you let us finish dessert first?" Cedar asked.

"You've had enough brownies." Tess set the pail on the floor with a clang. "I was using the facilities and noticed that the toilet-paper bucket was full. Time to burn it."

The brownie turned over in Tabitha's stomach. "Can't it go in the outhouse?"

Tess shook her head. "Because we're at such a high altitude and the area is so environmentally sensitive, we're not supposed to throw toilet paper in the outhouse. We burn it instead. The last people to use the hut didn't do their job, so we'll have to do it for them."

Cedar grinned. "Looks like it's Tabitha's turn to do it. She was the last one in the lake today."

Tabitha's jaw dropped. Cedar *was* as bad as Ashley. How could she have thought he was nice?

"You can all do it together," Tess said. "I'll do the dishes."

Cedar and Ashley glared at their mom. Tabitha almost laughed—they looked so much alike—until they turned their glare on her.

"Get going," Tess said.

Ashley and Cedar grabbed two kindling pieces each from beside the woodstove and used them to pick up the toilet paper and feed it into the fire. Tabitha did the same. It was the grossest thing she'd ever done. Why did anyone choose to go hiking? First you tortured yourself climbing straight up a mountain, then you took an ice bath, ate disgusting food and finished it off by watching someone's poo burn.

Ashley leaned nearer to Tabitha. "I wish you'd never come on this trip," she said.

Tabitha jerked back. The toilet paper fell off her sticks and onto the floor.

"Ash," Cedar warned.

"I'm serious," Ashley said. "This used to be a trip for the four of us, and now here you are instead of Dad. He'd never have let you on this trip. You're too weak to hike with us."

Tabitha threw the toilet paper into the fire. The injustice of what Ashley had said turned her insides into burning coals. "I didn't want to be here in the first place," she said. "My parents made me come. I wish I could go home—away from here and away from you."

Ashley raised her eyebrows. "Wouldn't that be nice."

Tabitha didn't bother replying. She brushed past Ashley and climbed the ladder to the loft.

CHAPTER THREE

Tabitha pulled on her pajamas while the rest of the family clomped around downstairs. Usually she peed before going to bed, but that would mean going back down through the hut again and going outside in her pj's. She decided to wait until morning to brush her teeth too. She rummaged through her pack for her headlamp, tucked it beside her and crawled into her sleeping bag.

As she'd done all summer, she put herself to sleep by reciting the Fibonacci string to herself. She had it memorized to 1597, but she still liked adding the numbers together in her head. 1+1=2. 1+2=3. 2+3=5. 3+5=8. Since she was little, she'd fallen asleep by counting, but the Fibonacci string was way more interesting than counting by twos. Ashley's and Cedar's voices drifted upstairs and broke her concentration.

"Did you hear about Jason's trip to Cerise Creek last year?" Ashley said.

"No."

"He was walking to the outhouse, and he heard something in the bushes. Guess what it was?"

"A bear?

"No, a snake!"

"Big deal," Cedar said.

"It was a rattler."

"Whatever," Cedar said.

Tabitha shivered in her sleeping bag. Could there be snakes way up at Lake Lovely Water? She hated snakes. 5+8=13. 8+13=21.

"I'm serious!" Ashley said.

"There aren't any rattlesnakes around here. Jason was lying."

"Mom, Cedar won't believe me. There are rattlesnakes in BC, right?"

"In the Interior. Not around here," Tess said.

"Well, maybe Jason was wrong about the rattler, but I'm sure he saw a snake."

Cedar snorted. "Right. Or maybe he thought he'd tell a good story."

Tabitha stuck her fingers in her ears to block out their voices. 13+21=34. Cedar must be right.

There couldn't be any snakes this high in the mountains. And definitely not any rattlers.

Once she shut out the noise from downstairs, it didn't take long to fall asleep—somewhere around 987. In the middle of the night she woke up and needed to pee so badly, it hurt. She lay there, tossing and turning, willing her body back to sleep. Squeezing her eyes shut, she tried to recite the Fibonacci string, but it didn't work.

She sat up and tried to unzip her sleeping bag quietly. Loud breathing ate up the air in the room. Tess's was the high-pitched whistling breath, Cedar's the rumbling followed by a snort and Ashley's—she paused. There wasn't a third breath.

"Watch for snakes," a low voice called from Ashley's bunk.

Tabitha froze. "There aren't any snakes. Nobody believes your story."

"How do you know? Maybe I'm right and they're all wrong. Maybe it's hiding in the outhouse, waiting to slither out and bite you."

Ashley was so full of it. Tabitha stalked to the ladder, no longer trying to be quiet. But as she climbed down, a cold feeling threaded its way from her stomach to her throat. What if there really was a snake hiding in the outhouse? She shook her head to get rid of the idea. Ashley was trying to scare her. She'd probably made up the whole story just so Tabitha would hear it.

The light from her headlamp flashed on Max, sleeping by the door. She grabbed her jacket. "Wake up and come with me." Max didn't move. "Let's go for a walk."

He labored to his feet, took a few steps away from the door and plopped back on the floor.

"Fine, I'll go by myself."

She started shivering the moment she stepped out the door. A mottled, inky sky loomed over her. No moon lit the path. Not even one star winked at her. She hurried to the outhouse, scanning back and forth with her headlamp.

The outhouse door squeaked as she pushed it open with her toe. She shone the light into the pit. Disgusting. But no snakes. She closed her eyes, held her breath and peed as fast as she could, imagining writhing serpents below her butt.

Her headlamp bounced on her head as she hurried back to the hut. Max's snores greeted her at the door.

"Night. Some help you were." She clambered up the ladder and into her sleeping bag.

Everyone else was sleeping. She closed her eyes and tried to sleep, but the fresh air and the fear left her wide awake.

Ping. Something clanged on the metal roof. She tensed, listening hard. More *pings.* Louder and faster.

Was the hut being attacked by squirrels? What if they found a hole in the roof and came looking for food?

Her body relaxed as she figured it out. Not squirrels, rain. A lot of rain by the sounds of it. The *pings* grew closer and closer, faster and faster, until they blended into a solid roar. She'd made it back from the outhouse just in time.

She groaned. Tess had planned for them to hike to a nearby peak the next day. Would she make them go in the rain? Which would be worse, hiking in the downpour or being stuck inside the hut all day? If they stayed inside, Ashley would spend the day reminding Tabitha that she didn't like her. She rolled over and tried to find a comfortable position. It was no use. The wooden slats of the bunk pushed through the thin foamie.

Finally she drifted off. Minutes later, it seemed, Tess got up and went downstairs to make tea. Cedar followed. Tabitha lifted her head and peered out the window. Gray fog stretched across the trees like cobwebs. She couldn't even see the outhouse, let alone the mountain ridges. She snuggled farther into her sleeping bag. Surely they wouldn't be going anywhere.

A teacup clinked on the wood table. "What are you doing up so early, Cedar?"

"Thought you'd want some company."

Tea poured into a second cup. "Just because your dad used to get up with me doesn't mean you have to."

"I was awake, that's all. And thirsty."

Silence for a moment. Tabitha imagined Cedar gulping hot tea.

Footsteps moved to the window. "No point in hiking to the ridge this morning," Tess said.

"The weather report looked good for the weekend."

"Bad timing," Tess said. "We need the rain though. And it'll make finding water easier on the way home."

It had been a hot, dry autumn. Tabitha's classroom at school was so hot that no one could concentrate, not even the teachers. Everyone had been grumpy.

Thinking about school made her grumpy, too, as she lay in her sleeping bag. She hadn't had a good start to the school year, thanks to Melissa Rogers. Even thinking her name made a knot twist in Tabitha's stomach.

"Nice shoes," Melissa had sneered as Tabitha sat at her desk on the first day of school. The girls sitting around Melissa—girls Tabitha had known most of her school life—giggled.

She was wearing the same runners she'd worn all summer. Pale blue. Used, but not ragged. Comfortable. She didn't think about them, she just put them on. Melissa and her giggling friends all wore ballet slippers decorated with shiny sequins.

"Do you have dance class today?" Tabitha asked, bringing on another fit of giggles.

"Where've you been all summer?" Melissa said. "Everybody's wearing ballet flats this year."

"Oh." She didn't bother telling them that she'd been at math camp in Manitoba for half of August.

Things got worse day by day. Girls snickered behind her back. Groups in the hallways broke apart as she approached. Kids pretended not to notice her. And no one told her what she'd done wrong, why she'd been singled out this year.

Over the summer almost every other girl in the class had grown breasts and an interest in makeup. Tabitha still had a flat chest and didn't own any makeup. She figured she made an easy target. But even when she tried to fit in by wearing some of her mom's lipstick to school, it didn't make a difference.

Getting out of bed in the morning became the hardest thing to do. Her mom had to force her to eat breakfast and make it to the bus on time. She even sent Tabitha to the school counselor, which only made things worse. The counselor told her everything would be confidential, but after they spoke, Melissa was called to the principal's office.

When she came back to the classroom, she made a detour past Tabitha's desk. "Snitch," she hissed.

After that, nobody talked to Tabitha anymore.

She overheard her mom on the phone with a friend. "Tabitha's depressed." Hearing that had made Tabitha feel even worse. She wanted to storm over to her mom and shout, "I am not!" But she couldn't force herself off the couch. Her parents had thought hiking with her cousins would make her feel better. Not likely.

Max woofed at the bottom of the ladder. At least he liked her. She unzipped her bag. There was no going back to sleep now.

"Morning, Tabitha," Tess said. "How'd you sleep?"

Tabitha gave Max a morning rub and kiss. "Okay. I'm not used to sleeping on a bunk. Or with other people around."

Tess nodded. "I remember the first time I slept in a hut. There were fifteen other people in it, and it was minus ten outside. One guy snored so loud I thought he'd start an avalanche, and another kept farting in his sleep."

Tabitha laughed. She couldn't imagine her parents ever saying something like that. In her family, they didn't fart; they were flatulent.

Max walked in circles by the door, wagging his tail and barking.

"Oh, *now* you want to go out, do you? All right." Tabitha grabbed her jacket and boots and turned to her aunt. "Do I need a leash?"

"No leash laws up here. Max is pretty good at staying nearby."

Cedar threw her a paper bag. "Catch. You'll need this."

Tabitha grabbed the bag off the floor where it had fallen. "What's this for?"

"Your pooper scooper."

She cringed. It was too late to back out of taking Max; he was wagging his tail and waiting for her at the door. "What do I do with it when it's full?"

"Empty it into the outhouse, then bring the bag back and we'll burn it," Tess said.

Tabitha sighed. She never knew there was so much poo involved in camping. "C'mon Max, let's get this over with."

As she opened the door, she caught a movement out of the corner of her eye. Ashley hung her head over the edge of the loft, smirking. Tabitha walked out the door. After it shut, she turned and stuck her tongue out in Ashley's direction.

The rain pelted her face and ran down the back of her neck. It was completely different outside than it had been the day before. Gray waves churned up the water, which looked dark and uninviting. She shivered at the thought of swimming in it. Even Max stayed away. He did his business by the path, and she scooped it up.

They ran to the outhouse. At least in daylight, she wasn't worried about snakes. She emptied the bag into the pit as quickly as she could, holding her breath.

"Let's go back, Max. Even spending time with Ashley is better than this."

Before this trip she hadn't seen Ashley for several months. Her cousins' house in Squamish was an hour's drive from Tabitha's home in Vancouver. Since Uncle Bruce's funeral, they hadn't seen much of each other, although Tabitha's mom had tried. She'd even tried to convince Tess to move to Vancouver and live with them for a while. Thank goodness Tess had rejected her mom's idea.

When Tabitha and her cousins were little, they used to play together all summer while Tess took classes to upgrade her midwifery degree. One time, Ashley and Tabitha played doctor. Of course, Ashley was always the doctor. Ashley had said Tabitha's belly button stuck out too much. To fix it she put a marble in it and told Tabitha to lie very still in the grass for half an hour. Tabitha lay on her back in the hot sun, trying not to let the marble roll out. Ashley was off playing with Cedar. After a while Tabitha's mom called them for lunch. Tabitha lay like a statue. Had it been half an hour? After the third call she got up, worrying as the marble rolled onto the grass.

"Where were you?" her mom asked, annoyed.

"In the backyard."

Ashley finished off her sandwich and grinned. "Is it an inny now?"

Not much had changed between them since.

CHAPTER FOUR

Inside the hut, Tess and Cedar were making oatmeal and tea for breakfast. Tabitha's stomach growled. Oatmeal sounded much better than curried chickpeas. She scooped up a huge bowl to make up for the night before.

"We won't be doing any hiking today," Tess said.

Tabitha nodded. She wasn't at all broken up about it. Her shoulders ached, and a blister on her heel was leaking clear liquid onto her sock. Her legs were so sore that each step made her wince. "It's really wet out there," she said.

"Rain's not the problem," Tess said. "We could get lost above the tree line in this fog."

"Are we going home early?" Tabitha tried to keep the hope out of her voice.

Cedar shook his head. "The weather forecast was for a decent weekend. Maybe tomorrow it'll be clear enough to scatter Dad's ashes on the ridge."

Tabitha's heart sank. She nodded.

Tess pulled a box off the shelf and handed it to Cedar. "Why don't you guys play Monopoly?"

"Not me," Ashley said. "I'm going back to bed."

"I'll play." Cedar turned to Tabitha. "You in?"

"Sure." It wasn't like she had anything else to do. Ashley paused as though she wanted to change her mind, then climbed the ladder to the loft.

"You playing, Mom?" Cedar asked.

Tess grabbed the ax from beside the stove. "No, I'll go chop some firewood."

Cedar let the box clatter onto the table. "I was going to do that later."

Tess shook her head. "I can handle it."

"But I want to."

"You don't have to do everything he did, Cedar."

"I just wanted to chop the wood," he said.

"I need exercise. You can chop more later." Tess marched out the door.

Cedar stared at the door for a moment, then shook his shoulders and started setting up the board and counting out the money.

Tabitha remembered Cedar at Uncle Bruce's funeral. The ceremony had been on a rock bluff overlooking Squamish—one of Bruce's favorite climbing spots. The guests wore T-shirts and shorts, and person after person spoke about Bruce's climbing career, his passion for life and his strong work ethic.

Tabitha had stood on tiptoes to see Cedar and Ashley as their faces floated in and out of view between the heads of people in front of her. Ashley's back was to Tess. She pulled away from her mom's arm, clinging to Cedar as the tears streamed down her face.

Cedar stood with a straight back, staring at the cliffs. Every once in a while, he had rolled his shoulders up to his ears and let them fall.

As the ceremony ended and the crowd moved down the hillside, three different people hugged Cedar and commented on how much he looked like his father. With each comment, Cedar had grown a little taller, his back a little straighter, and the deep lines between his eyebrows had eased.

Now Tabitha chose the thimble as her Monopoly piece—it was solid and wouldn't roll off the table—and put it on *GO*. She worried she'd do something dumb like knock all the pieces on the floor and then Cedar would stop playing with her.

"You go first," he said. "You're the youngest."

She frowned. He and Ashley always made such a big deal about that.

Cedar's mouth pulled up on one side. "We always play youngest goes first."

"Oh." She rolled the dice and moved her thimble to St. Charles Place. "I'll buy a house."

"That'll be a hundred and forty bucks."

She handed over the money.

"You always this quiet?" Cedar asked.

Tabitha's cheeks flushed. "I don't know."

Cedar rolled and moved his die. He landed on St. Charles Place and groaned.

She grinned. "That's ten dollars."

He passed her a ten, and she rolled again.

After several minutes of playing, he said, "So, how come you're so quiet?"

She sighed. Couldn't he let her be? "My family's quieter than yours, I guess."

"Are you this quiet with your friends?"

She shrugged and rolled the dice. What friends?

"Mom said you were having trouble at school," Cedar said.

Tabitha's jaw clenched. Mothers were all the same. They didn't know how to keep their mouths shut. "I'll buy the Short Line Railroad."

"You won't have enough to pay me rent."

"On what? You only own two properties, and they're on the other side of the board."

Cedar grinned and pulled on his ponytail. "I might buy something next turn."

"I'll take the chance."

"You're gutsier than I thought," he said.

Smiling to herself, she passed over another $200. She only had $62 left, but she'd be passing *GO* soon. As long as he didn't leapfrog past her, she'd be okay.

"So are you?" he asked.

"What?"

"Having problems at school."

Her cheeks had cooled off as they played. Now they flushed again. "It's all right."

"That's not how it sounded. What's wrong? Bad teacher?"

She sighed. "The other kids don't like me."

Cedar stared out the window. "I know something about that."

"Right." He had to be one of the cool kids.

"Ashley and I aren't exactly part of the popular crowd."

Tabitha shook the dice between her cupped hands. She always used to think he and Ashley were cool. They seemed so sure of themselves. But if she really thought about it, not one boy in her school wore a ponytail like Cedar's. And none of the girls chose to go hiking with their parents on the weekend. Maybe they had problems at school she'd never dreamed of. "You guys seem happy."

He ran a hand across his hair. "I don't let things bother me."

"Like what?"

"Kids call me 'nature freak' and 'girlie,' and worse. If they think it doesn't bother you, they stop." He picked up the dice and went back to the game.

Tess opened the door and walked in with a load of wood. She stacked it by the fire. Then she sat down with a book, the first time she'd sat still since they'd arrived at the hut. She used to sit around more when Bruce was alive. Did she need to work twice as hard now that Bruce was gone, or was she trying to keep herself busy?

A couple of hours later Tabitha had hotels on three properties and houses on seven. She owned the electric company and all four railroads. Cedar would be bankrupt in a few more turns.

"How's the game?" Tess asked.

"Tabitha's way too good at this." Cedar didn't sound upset. He rolled and landed on Atlantic Avenue.

Tabitha grinned. "That's another eight hundred and fifty dollars. Do you have enough?"

Ashley hopped down the ladder into the kitchen. She stood over the table with her hands on her hips.

"You guys are *still* playing? Don't you have anything better to do?"

"Like sleep all morning?" Cedar said. "You should have played. Might have learned a few things."

Ashley scrunched up her face. "What do you mean?"

"Tabitha can add all the money in her head, and knows what change to give without having to count it out."

Tabitha bit her lip to keep from smiling.

Ashley eyed Tess in the chair. In a loud voice, she said, "That's good." Then she leaned over and put her mouth close to Tabitha's ear. "At least there's one thing you're good at."

Tabitha stared right into her eyes, determined not to show her that the comment hurt. Maybe if she followed Cedar's advice, Ashley would give up.

Ashley squeezed beside Cedar on the bench. "Want to take Max for a walk?"

"We're almost finished," he said. "I'll meet you when I'm done."

Ashley jumped up as though she'd realized the bench was burning hot. She put on her jacket. "Don't bother. You and Tabitha can have a nice time together." She stomped out the door and slammed it shut.

Tess shook her head. "Teenage hormones."

Tabitha rolled her eyes. Adults could be so dense.

They spent a long stuffy day inside, listening to the rain. Ashley came back from her walk before lunch and started doing a puzzle by the fire. By late afternoon, Tabitha couldn't take being cooped up for one minute longer. "Let's go outside, Max."

"Don't go alone," Tess said. "You could get lost in the fog."

Tabitha stopped, her hand on the door. "I went out this morning."

"The fog's lower now, and it'll be dark soon," she said. She tapped Ashley's shoulder. "You can keep Tabitha company."

Ashley's head sprang up from the puzzle. "I've already been out."

"More fresh air won't kill you," Tess said. "And Max needs another walk." Max thumped his tail on the floor as if agreeing.

"Why don't you make Cedar go?" Ashley said.

Cedar was stretched out on the bench, dozing. Tess looked at her.

"Dad wouldn't have made me go," she said.

Tess flinched as though the words had been a slap in the face. She narrowed her eyes and said, "You're going."

Ashley grabbed her jacket. "Let's make this quick."

"Fine," Tabitha muttered.

CHAPTER FIVE

Evening was already descending as they walked out the door. The low gray clouds made it gloomy even at four in the afternoon. Wet bushes rustled in the wind, sprinkling water over their legs as they brushed past. The lake was even more forbidding now, the color of the water in the school janitor's mop bucket. Tabitha pulled up the hood on her jacket and cinched the cord tight, trying to keep the wind from blowing the rain down her neck.

Max bounded ahead, then circled back. He reminded her so much of Bruce. Even on a short walk to the swimming pool, her uncle used to circle among the kids, trying to contain his extra energy. Everyone knew he wanted to yell, "Hurry up!" Barrel-chested, with a deep, booming voice and a curly blond beard, Bruce was passionate about mountaineering. Tabitha had never understood what he loved about climbing frozen mountains. It was bad enough hiking in dry weather.

People said he died doing what he loved, as though that made it okay that his kids no longer had a father and that Tess had lost her husband. While crossing an ice field on a mountain up north, he'd fallen into a crevasse—a giant crack in the ice. When the rest of his group pulled him out, he was already dead. He'd hit his head in the fall. Max had sat by the front window of their house for weeks, waiting for Bruce to come home.

Tabitha shook her head to get rid of the sad thoughts. "Let's walk to the far side of the lake."

"We'll never make it in this weather," Ashley said.

Tabitha kept walking. "Watch me," she whispered to herself. She'd had enough of Ashley telling her what to do. Enough of Ashley making her feel like a little kid. Enough of standing back and taking it.

The rain pelted her face. The path was hard to see in the fog. Partway along, they came to a rock field. The trail disappeared, and large boulders blocked their path. She could barely make out an orange marker on a rock a few steps away.

Max sniffed and leaped among the rocks. Tabitha followed, lurching from one boulder to another, using her hands for balance.

"Can't you go faster?" Ashley asked.

"Go in front if you're so fast."

Ashley pushed past her on the next large rock and almost knocked her over. As her cousin leaped from rock to rock, Tabitha tried to follow but wasn't as sure of herself, especially on the slippery surfaces of the boulders.

"It's not a race," she said.

Ashley spun around on one foot and said in a sing-song voice, "Is the wittle baby getting tired?"

Before Tabitha could respond, Ashley spun back and jumped for the next rock. As she did, her back foot slipped out from under her. Her body landed flat across two rocks, and her cheek whacked the stone.

Tabitha winced.

Ashley lay still.

"Nice try," Tabitha said. "You can't fool me."

Her cousin didn't move. Tabitha crossed her arms and waited. Ashley continued to lie there. Tabitha leaned over her. It didn't even sound like she was breathing. "Are you okay?" she asked. "What's wrong?"

Ashley took a gasping breath and groaned. She cried out as she tried to push herself up off the rocks. Her hand was slippery with blood. "Help me up."

Tabitha grabbed Ashley around the chest and heaved her upright. She was heavy for someone so thin. Max pushed his way through and nuzzled

40

Ashley's legs. Tabitha tried to nudge him out of the way, but he wouldn't move from Ashley's side.

A circle of white skin pulsated on Ashley's cheek. Blood dripped from her hand. Ashley raised her clean hand to her cheek and gasped as her fingers grazed the skin. Tears poured down her cheeks.

Tabitha gulped. Ashley's right cheek, the one she'd fallen on, looked flatter than the left side. "I think we'd better go back."

"Yeah." The word came out muffled, like Ashley had a cold.

"Can you walk back to the hut?" Tabitha asked.

Ashley took a few shuddering breaths. "I guess." She didn't move. "My mom's gonna be so mad."

"Why? You fell."

Ashley pressed her hands together to try and stop the bleeding. "She'll know I was showing off."

Tabitha began picking her way through the rocks. "How will she know?"

"Duh. When you tell her," she said.

"Have I ever told on you before?"

"You did when I pushed you into the mud."

Tabitha's fingers dug into her hands as she clenched her fists. "I was four!"

Ashley wrinkled her forehead. "I guess you're right."

Tabitha continued along the trail. Ashley walked with her hands pressed together as though she was praying.

The light was starting to fade. Tabitha shivered in her light jacket as the wind whipped off the lake.

"Can you slow down?" Ashley said.

Tabitha turned, surprised to see that her cousin had fallen behind. She waited for her to catch up. "Are you okay? Should I get help?"

"I can make it. But not so fast." Ashley's face had turned gray, and blood was starting to drip from her hand again.

Tabitha wished they'd brought the first-aid kit.

As much as she'd hated hiking, it had never occurred to her that it could be dangerous. Bad things were only supposed to happen to people who took risks, like Bruce on the steep ice fields.

Even though Tabitha felt sorry for Ashley, a tiny part of her was happy to know that her cousin wasn't as tough as she appeared. And maybe, now that she recognized that Tabitha was no longer four, she'd stop treating her like a little kid.

Max trotted ahead and then ran back, circling their legs. When the hut came into view, he raced toward it and waited on the front step.

Cedar whistled as they pushed open the door. "Ouch."

"What happened?" Tess asked, rushing for her first-aid kit.

"Ashley slipped on a boulder," Tabitha said.

Cedar peered at her cheek. "What were you doing on the rocks?"

"I wanted to walk to the other side of the lake," Tabitha said.

Tess elbowed Cedar out of the way. "Not such a good idea in this weather."

"Yeah," Ashley said. "And then she wanted to race. That's when I slipped."

Tess looked at Tabitha with disappointment. "You shouldn't take chances in this weather."

Tabitha stood open-mouthed. She couldn't believe Ashley had lied. But then, why should she be surprised, really? She pursed her lips and stared at her cousin, who wouldn't meet her eye.

Tess sat Ashley in the chair by the fire and put on her headlamp. Ashley jerked back when she prodded her cheek. "That hurts!"

Good, thought Tabitha.

"I think you might have broken a bone," Tess said. She'd worked for twenty years as a midwife. A broken bone was probably no big deal to her. Her voice stayed calm and controlled. "Open and close your mouth."

Ashley did as she was told, but her jaw only opened a fraction, and her teeth didn't meet properly when she closed her mouth. Tess patted her fingers under Ashley's eye. "What do you feel?"

"Nothing."

Tess nodded. "I'm pretty sure it's broken." She turned off the headlamp and sat back on her heels.

Cedar sat on the bench and leaned toward Ashley. "Is it serious?"

"We need to get her to a hospital. They probably won't do anything, but we need an X-ray. Sometimes broken cheekbones need surgery. And she won't be able to eat."

"So we're going home early," Cedar said.

Tess nodded. "First thing tomorrow." She pulled some swabs from her first-aid kit and cleaned Ashley's hand. Then she wrapped it in a bandage.

Ashley sat on the bench and watched the other three prepare dinner. Tabitha didn't feel as awkward as she had the night before. As she stirred the noodles in the pot, she turned her back to her cousin. Even looking at Ashley made her seethe inside. She knew she should feel sorry for her. She must be in a lot of pain. But obviously not so much pain that she couldn't lay the blame on Tabitha.

Ashley sat quietly through dinner. She couldn't eat the noodles. Tess had made her a mug of soup, but even that was difficult for her to manage.

Tess motioned out the window. "We probably would have been heading home tomorrow anyway, with this weather."

Cedar frowned. "It might clear, and then we could hike to the ridge." He waved a fork at Tabitha. "Couldn't you guys have used your brains?"

Tabitha stabbed her spaghetti. It was so unfair. If she defended herself now, they'd think she was lying or trying to get out of trouble.

"Oh, let it drop," Tess said. "What's done is done."

"Yeah," Ashley said. Her words were muffled, but her tone was sickly sweet. "You'll be more careful next time, won't you, Tabitha?"

That was too much. Tabitha pushed her half-eaten bowl of noodles to Cedar. "You finish these. Something's making me sick." She swung her legs off the stool and ran out the door. At least tonight she knew enough to use the outhouse before she went to bed.

CHAPTER SIX

Tabitha lay in her sleeping bag listening to the rain beat on the roof. During the day, the sound of the rain disappeared in the mix of voices, pots and pans rattling, and boots stomping. At night the raindrops beating on the roof consumed all the other noises. It felt like a drum banging on her head. The only good thing was that it drowned out Cedar's snoring.

She rolled over and tried to get back to sleep. After storming off at dinnertime, she'd had no choice but to go to bed early. Now, in the middle of the night, she wasn't tired.

Ashley moaned in her sleep. Tabitha hoped she was having a nightmare.

"Stop!" Ashley called out.

Tabitha raised her head. Her cousin rolled over and mumbled. She was still asleep.

"Dad, come back!" Her voice sounded frantic. Tabitha could just make out Ashley's flailing arms. She had a pretty good idea what the nightmare was about, and she wouldn't wish that on anybody, not even Ashley.

Ashley had glowered throughout Bruce's funeral. Whenever anyone tried to hug her, she'd stiffened, refusing to hug them back. Tabitha wondered if Ashley's anger would ever end. Tabitha's mom said time healed everything. After listening to Ashley's nightmare, she wondered how much time it would take. Forever?

Eventually Ashley settled down, and the sound of the rain took over the room again. Tomorrow they were going home. Tabitha smiled in the dark. Off the mountain, back to civilization.

When Tess woke them the next morning, the rain was coming down harder than ever. Outside the window, all was gray. They were living inside a cloud.

Tabitha pulled on her damp clothes and stuffed her sleeping bag into its sack. Tess handed her a plastic garbage bag. "Line your pack with this. It'll help keep everything dry."

Tabitha did as Tess suggested, but she didn't know why she bothered. Even the sleeping bag felt wet, as though the mist had permeated the walls of the hut.

She gulped down a big breakfast of oatmeal and granola, hoping the sooner she finished, the sooner they'd be on their way home. Ashley ate nothing, once again. Tess held a mug of hot chocolate up to her mouth, and she managed a few sips. Cedar ate his cereal and reached for the trail mix, but Tess put a hand on his wrist to stop him.

"C'mon," he said. "We've got tons of food left. No way I'm going to carry it all home."

Tess shoved the trail mix into a bag and pulled the cord tight. "We still have to hike all the way down and cross the river. It's smart to carry extra food."

"Don't you remember Dad's rule?" Ashley said it like an accusation.

Cedar sighed. "Of course I remember. *A camper who plans well comes home with food to spare.*" He tipped his mug of hot chocolate into his mouth and licked around the edge. "But we're on the way home. We won't need it."

Tess turned her back to Cedar and packed the rest of the food. They washed their dishes and cleaned up the hut, letting Max do a last scour for crumbs.

Cedar lifted the box with Bruce's ashes off the shelf. "We haven't scattered Dad's ashes yet."

Tess took a deep breath. "Right. Let's go to the lake before we start down the mountain."

Ashley shook her head. "We're spreading them on the ridge. On his favorite lookout."

"But we can't make it up there today. You know that," Tess said.

"Then bring them home. I'm not throwing them any old place. And they'll clump together in the rain."

Tabitha shuddered at the image of clumps of Bruce's ashes melting in the rain on the lakeshore.

Tess sighed. "Fine. We'll bring him home again."

"And then what?" Cedar asked.

"We'll come back in the spring."

Cedar's shoulders slumped as Ashley's lips lifted in a small smile. Tabitha couldn't believe she'd want to come back. But then, if it were her dad, she'd probably want to hold on to him in any way she could, not toss him off some mountain ridge.

Tess took the ashes from Cedar and put them in her pack. With a last look around to make sure the hut was tidy, she led them out the door.

Tabitha still had bruises on her shoulders from carrying her pack two days before. She thought it would be much lighter after eating all the food, but it still felt full of rocks. At least they would be hiking downhill.

The trail down turned out to be treacherous, almost worse than the way up. After three days of rain, it was like walking through a muddy river. On the way up they'd used the roots to help pull themselves along. Now the roots were slick with mud, useless for gripping and a hazard if stepped on. Tabitha fell so many times, she looked like she'd been wading through a sewer. She was drenched from her ballcap to the laces of her boots before they made it to the first creek. Even Max slipped and slid. His hair hung in brown mats from his belly.

They didn't have to worry about finding water to drink. The dried-up creek beds they'd crossed on the way up had turned into frothing streams. The wooden boards they'd used as small bridges were all under water. With no easy way around, they had to splash right through. Tabitha didn't think it possible, but her feet got even wetter than before, and colder too.

"Why don't they build bridges over these creeks?" she asked.

"They aren't usually this full," Tess said. "Remember how dry they were two days ago?"

Tabitha had imagined the way home would be faster than the way up, but it still felt like forever. Finally, after sloshing through a stream up to her knees, she turned a corner and heard rushing water. It was way louder than the sound of any of the creeks.

"We're almost there," she yelled.

"Uh-huh," Tess said. "The river sounds pretty loud."

Tabitha heard a note of worry in her aunt's voice. "What if it's too rough?" she asked.

Ashley snorted. "Scared of water? You can't get any wetter than you already are."

"I see you're feeling better," Tabitha retorted.

Before Ashley could answer, Tess, who'd walked ahead, called out, "Oh, dear god."

They ran over a rise to see what she was talking about. Before them was the Squamish River. Only it didn't look like a river. It was a churning, roiling lake, twice as big as when they'd last seen it. Huge trees spun in the chocolate brown water. The forest looked like a primeval swamp, with trees growing out of the water and everything shrouded in a heavy mist.

"Still think that'll be easy to cross?" Tabitha asked.

Ashley's face turned whiter than it already was. "Where's our canoe?"

Tabitha scanned the water. Surely this wasn't the same place they'd started their hike.

"Did we come down a different part of the trail?" she asked.

"No, stupid," Ashley said. "There's only one trail."

Tess didn't even notice the exchange. She was too busy frowning at the water. "The river's come up several meters since we left. Our canoe's out there somewhere." She pointed across the swirling current.

Tabitha edged closer to the water.

"Don't get too close," Tess warned. "The current's strong."

The river swirled trees around like a hose washing twigs off the sidewalk. Tabitha stepped back. They weren't going to rescue the canoe, even if they could see it through the mucky water.

"What are we going to do?" Cedar asked.

"Can we call someone? I have my cell phone," Tabitha said.

Tess shook her head. "There's no service anywhere on this side of the river. Even if we could call, no one would be able to cross that." She motioned toward the trail with her chin. "Looks like the only thing we can do is go back to the hut."

Ashley, Tabitha and Cedar groaned.

"But we just hiked all the way down!" Ashley said.

"Can't we camp here?" Cedar asked.

"No," Tess said. "We don't have tents. And we don't know how long we'll have to wait for a rescue. Wouldn't you rather be in a dry hut with a stove while we're waiting?"

The situation was serious. Tabitha could see that. They couldn't strap together rafts of tree trunks and float their way to safety, even though she imagined her cousins doing something like that. They were stuck until the river dropped.

Rain still poured from the sky. Who knew how long it would be until they could get back?

"My parents are going to be so worried," she said.

"Not till tomorrow," Tess said. "We weren't planning on coming home until then."

"Right," Tabitha said.

Ashley cradled her cheek with her hand. "No one will think to look for us for two days."

"Mm-hmm." Tess stepped off the trail into the woods. "Let's stop and rest before we walk back up. It will be drier under these trees."

Tabitha followed Tess, then dropped her pack and sat on it. The one good thing about the rain was that it kept the mosquitoes away. She didn't have to swat anything except the water droplets falling in her eyes.

Tess pulled out the stove.

"We're cooking?" Tabitha asked.

"I thought some soup might cheer us up." Tess opened her food sack.

Tabitha pulled the hood of her rain jacket over her head and crouched into as small a ball as possible. Tess seemed so calm. Why wasn't she more worried? They might be stuck over here forever.

Cedar grabbed the pot and filled it with water from a nearby stream that flowed into the main river. Tabitha was glad they didn't have to take it from the muddy torrent below them.

She stared at the water as the soup cooked. It mesmerized her, like looking into a fire. She imagined her mom and dad at home. They were probably curled up on the living room couch, cozy and warm. She'd give anything to be back there. Before she left, she'd yelled at them. "I hate you guys. You're making me go on this trip to get me out of the house. Because you can't wait to get rid of me."

Her mom sighed. "You know that isn't true. You're having such a tough time right now—"

"And you can't stand having me around!"

"And you'll have fun on the hike. You need to spend time with kids your age."

Tabitha turned her back to her mother. "That's what I do at school. And nobody likes me."

Her mom tried to comfort her by putting her arm around her shoulder. "Ashley and Cedar aren't like the kids at school."

Tabitha brushed her arm away. "That's what you think."

Her mom had been right. Her cousins were nothing like the kids at school. But that didn't mean they were nice to be around. And what made her mom think camping was fun?

How would her parents feel when she didn't come home? Guilty for sending her? Relieved that they had another day to themselves? No. Deep down she knew the truth. They really had been trying to help, even if it hadn't worked. They'd be worried sick.

Tess poured hot tomato soup into mugs, snapping Tabitha out of her reverie. Ashley leaned in and grabbed hers. The whole side of her face was beginning to swell. She looked half human, half chipmunk. She held her soup to her lips, but Tabitha didn't see her swallow. How would her cousin find the energy to climb back up the mountain? For that matter, how would she?

CHAPTER SEVEN

The soup warmed her, but even so, she didn't feel ready to run up the trail, which looked like a dark mouth waiting to gobble them up.

Tess stood and wiped her cup with a finger. "Time to get moving, guys. No sense sitting around in the rain."

Silently they wiped their cups, packed them away, and shouldered their bags. How many steps until they reached the hut? Three thousand? Three million? Tabitha tried counting, but lost her place every time she came to a slippery section. Was that four hundred or five hundred? Even Max was tired. He padded dolefully beside her. Sometimes he crossed in front of her and stopped.

She bumped into his rear end. "Max, keep moving."

His face sagged, as if he were saying, *Can't we rest for a second?*

"It's not up to me," Tabitha said. "Besides, hanging around here won't help." She pushed him in the rump. He dropped his head and moved forward again, letting out a loud sigh.

Tabitha and Ashley reached the next creek ahead of Cedar and Tess. When they'd crossed it on the way down, the water had reached their knees. Tabitha couldn't decide if it was her imagination, but it seemed like the water had risen even farther. Compared to most of the other creeks, this one looked calm. Only a few rocks broke its surface. But the water moved swiftly.

Before stepping in, Ashley unbuckled her pack.

"Why are you doing that?" Tabitha asked.

Ashley turned and rolled her eyes. "So I can get out of it if I fall in, of course." Tabitha nodded and undid her strap. She was too tired to care about Ashley's attitude.

Her cousin stepped in and sank to mid-thigh. Tabitha followed, gasping as the icy water shocked her system. She shuddered, frozen to the core from one step. Ashley pushed her leg through the water again. Now the water reached her waist.

"Maybe we should turn around," Tabitha called.

Ashley shook her head. "Nowhere else to go but up." As she lifted her foot, her body shifted. The water lifted her off her feet. She plunged into the current, her backpack dragging her under.

"Ashley!" Tabitha threw off her pack and lunged for her. She managed to grab a strap of Ashley's pack, but lost her footing. Her boots slipped and she landed on her butt on a rock. Waves slapped her face and threatened to pull her under. She grabbed the nearest boulder and pushed herself to standing.

But it wasn't it a boulder. It was Ashley's pack. Only Ashley was no longer attached to it. "Where are you?" Tabitha tried to keep her panic down and her feet steady as she searched for Ashley.

"Here!" Ashley's faint voice floated from down-stream. Tabitha saw her clinging to a log in the middle of the creek. She must have slipped out of her pack while Tabitha was holding it.

Tabitha stepped farther into the stream.

"Stop!" Ashley called. "You'll get swept away too!"

Tabitha didn't listen. Ashley must be freezing. Where were Tess and Cedar? If they didn't get her out soon, she might die of hypo-whatever it was. She heaved Ashley's pack onto the bank and stepped back into the stream, trying to see her footing through the deep water. Another step. She wobbled in the current, but managed to hold herself up. *Don't fall. Don't fall.*

"Tabitha, stop!" a voice called from behind her.

She slowly turned and saw Tess, white-faced, on the bank.

"We have a rope! Don't go any farther." She grabbed a large stick and held it out to Tabitha.

Tabitha took hold of the stick and pulled herself out of the water as Tess continued to give instructions. "Ashley, we'll be there in a sec! Cedar, open my pack and get the rope."

Cedar dropped his own pack on the ground and opened Tess's. He rummaged through it and came out holding a yellow coil. He tied one end around a tree and grabbed the other end.

As Tabitha's feet found dry ground, Tess turned and saw Cedar. "What are you doing? I'm going to get her."

Cedar shook his head. "No you aren't. I can do this."

"You're too young. Let me go."

"I'm ready. Hold the rope and I'll go get her."

"Cedar, don't. I'm the one who should do this."

Cedar's back stiffened. He turned and glared at his mom. "I'm old enough and strong enough. I'm doing it."

Tess took a deep breath, then nodded and picked up the slack rope close to where Cedar stood. "I'll pay out the rope from here. Tying the rope to the tree is good backup, but you'd still be swept down the river if you fell."

Tabitha's teeth chattered. "Why do you need slack? Why not just tie the rope closer to the tree?"

"He needs enough slack to move around and get Ashley, but not so much that he'll float a long way if he falls. Also, once he gets Ashley, we'll have to set a line across the whole creek."

Cedar walked to the edge of the creek closest to Ashley. "Hold on, I'm coming to get you."

"Wait!" Tabitha called.

Cedar stopped. He and Tess swiveled to look at her.

"You need to choose another tree. The angle's wrong with that one. If Cedar falls, the water will sweep him too far downstream, and then we'll have to get both of them!"

Tess frowned. Tabitha held her breath, waiting for her aunt to tell her off for slowing down the rescue. For once her math skills would be useful for something other than a board game, if only her aunt would listen to her.

"You're right," Tess said. She untied the rope, moved it to a tree farther upstream and looked to Tabitha for approval. "That better?"

Tabitha nodded.

"Let's get going," Tess called to Cedar.

"Hurry!" Ashley yelled.

Cedar splashed through the water, fighting to stay upright. Tess braced herself on the bank, dug her feet into the ground, leaned back slightly and let the rope ease through her hands as he moved forward.

Tabitha shivered on the riverbank, clutching Max. Just a few seconds in the river had frozen her. How was Ashley surviving so long?

Finally Cedar reached her. He grabbed her arm and pulled her through the water. Together they slipped and slid over the rocks. Twice, Ashley's feet went out from under her. Only Cedar's grip kept her from being swept downstream. They reached the other side of the bank, and Ashley collapsed onto the ground. Cedar tied the rope around a tree.

"I'll take your pack," Tess said to Tabitha. "Cross to the other side quickly."

Tabitha nodded and did as she was told. The last thing she wanted to do was to get back into the icy river, but she was so cold now, it didn't really make a difference. The water slammed into her legs as she picked her way across. She held onto the rope and managed to make it without slipping.

Tess and Cedar each made two trips with the packs. On the final trip, Tess untied the rope from the tree and retied it around her waist. Cedar gathered the slack as she crossed. Soon they all huddled on the far side of the bank.

"Get out some dry clothes, you two," Tess said.

Tabitha dropped her pack and started pulling out clothes. Thanks to the garbage bag, her clothes weren't soaked through. She was so cold, she didn't even care that Cedar was there as she stripped off her shirt and put on a drier fleece. Ashley nodded but didn't move.

"Cedar, get some clothes for your sister," Tess said. She began pulling off Ashley's clothes and then hugged her in a tight embrace. Cedar handed her the dry clothes, and Tess put them on her, then hugged her again. Within a few minutes, Ashley seemed to revive a bit.

"Thanks," she said to Cedar.

He shrugged. "No big deal."

Tess peered at Ashley's face. "How does it feel?"

"It aches," she said.

Tess pulled out her first-aid kit and handed Ashley a white pill. "Take this painkiller."

Ashley looked at the pill in her hand. "You always tell us not to take these."

"I don't make a habit of using drugs for no reason, but this is a special case."

Ashley stared at the pill. "I can't swallow it."

"Just take it," Cedar said.

Ashley shook her head. "I mean, I can't swallow pills like this. They get stuck in my throat. Don't we have any of the little-kid ones? Or some jam I can eat it with?"

Tabitha coughed to cover a snort. Amazon-girl Ashley was scared to swallow a pill? She'd have to eat twelve little-kid pills to make up for an adult one.

She started to make a nasty comment, but stopped when she saw the misery on her cousin's face. "Put it way back on your tongue, take a sip of water and throw your head back."

Ashley grimaced, then opened her mouth a crack and dropped the pill in. She gagged a bit, but managed to get it down. "Thanks."

"Let's get going," Tess said. "We need to make a fire and get everyone warm."

They nodded and shouldered their packs.

CHAPTER EIGHT

The hike to the hut was painful. They slipped and fell and groaned. Tabitha cried more than once, but at least the rain streaming down her cheeks hid her tears. They crossed four more creeks that had turned from trickles to torrents with the rain. Tess and Cedar took turns setting the rope. Tabitha and Ashley were too worn out to want to try setting the safety lines.

Each time she crossed a creek, Tabitha had to steel herself before taking the first step into the water. Her feet knew how cold, slippery and dangerous it would be, and she had to talk them into leaving the bank. Her hands gripped the rope so tightly that she had to force them to unclench and mover farther up the safety line. Four times she splashed through water up to her waist.

Four times she made it across and collapsed onto the bank.

They reached the lake at dusk. The rain still fell and the clouds hung low and gray. If she hadn't already been there, Tabitha never would have believed the lake was surrounded by mountain peaks. The oppressive gray reflected her mood. She'd never felt so tired in her life. Even going to school and facing Melissa would be better than being stuck up there in the rain.

Cedar led the way as they trudged the last few steps to the hut. Max plodded behind, his fur so wet he looked more like a river otter than a dog. By the time Tabitha got inside, Cedar was starting a fire.

"Try to find some dry clothes, and I'll get started on dinner," Tess said.

"Good, I'm starving," Cedar said.

By the time Tabitha came down and hung her wet clothes by the fire, Tess had started boiling water on the stove.

"Can I help?" Tabitha asked.

"There's not much to do," Tess said. "All we're having is noodles."

"That's it?" Cedar asked. "But I'm so hungry."

Tess pressed her lips into a line. "We're all hungry, but we don't know how long we'll be here and we need to save our food."

"You mean we might run out?" Tabitha asked.

"I'm sure that won't happen." But Tess didn't meet Tabitha's eyes as she said it.

Nobody spoke during dinner. It took all of Tabitha's strength to lift her spoon to her mouth. Plain noodles with salt and pepper had never tasted so good. Ashley stared at her cup of tea, but didn't make a move to drink.

"You need to get fluid in your body," Tess said.

Ashley nodded, but didn't do anything.

Tess sat beside her and lifted the cup to her mouth. "Drink," she ordered.

Ashley took a small sip.

Tess handed Cedar and Tabitha one square of chocolate each for dessert. Tabitha cradled it in her hand like a precious gem. Resisting the urge to stuff the whole thing down her throat, she let the square sit on her tongue for as long as possible, savoring the taste. The sweet chocolate oozed through her mouth. She rolled her tongue around, relishing the smooth yumminess of it.

For the first time since the trip started, Tabitha slept through the night. The sound of the rain actually soothed her. It had become such a constant noise, she hardly noticed it anymore.

She woke the next morning to rustling and murmuring. Lifting her head a few inches, she saw that Ashley and Cedar still slept. It must be Tess downstairs.

"It's going to be a long day."

Tabitha lay back on her bunk and listened. Who was she talking to? Max?

"I know, I know. It could be more than that."

It sounded like she was talking on the phone and Tabitha could only hear one half of the conversation, but Tess had said phones didn't work up here. Otherwise they would have called for help already.

"Yeah, maybe up to a week."

Tabitha almost fell off her bunk as the words sank in. A week? What would they eat? What would her parents do?

Who was Tess talking to?

"I miss you too."

Now Tabitha was really confused. Who could Tess be missing? The only person she could think of was Bruce, but there's no way she could be talking to him—unless his ghost had come to visit. As quietly as she could, she slipped out of her sleeping bag and padded to the ladder. Peering over, she saw Tess cradling her teacup and staring at the box of Bruce's ashes.

As Tabitha climbed down, Tess jerked her head in surprise, then recovered and smiled.

"Morning. I didn't know anyone was up."

"Any tea left?" Tabitha asked.

Tess pointed to the pot. "I found a stash of tea on the shelf. That's one thing we don't have to conserve."

Tabitha poured herself a mug of tea. She opened her mouth to ask if Tess always talked to Bruce, then shut it again. It was obviously something private. If she wanted to talk to ghosts, that was her choice.

She sipped her tea and rinsed it around in her mouth. Her teeth felt furry. Her scalp itched. Her body stank. It had been three days since her brief swim in the lake. The fall in the river hadn't done much to clean her.

"I wish I could shower," she said.

Tess smiled. "You could go stand in the rain."

"What did you do on the big ten-day trips you and Bruce used to take?" As soon as she asked, she worried that she'd made a mistake. Would it bother Tess to talk about Bruce?

But Tess only shrugged and said, "We'd try to swim a few times. Being dirty doesn't bother me. In fact, I think bathing is a waste of time and water. I only shower every three or four days at home."

Tabitha's jaw dropped. Ever since she was a little kid, she'd had a bath or a shower almost every day. So did her parents. She loved being clean.

Footsteps padded across the sleeping loft, and Ashley's face appeared at the top of the ladder. The swelling on her face had turned purple, and her chipmunk cheek was even more pronounced. She slowly made her way down the ladder and sat beside Tess.

"Tea?" her mom asked.

Ashley shook her head. Tess held the cup to her mouth anyway.

Cedar jumped down the ladder. "I'm starving, what's for breakfast?"

"Granola," Tess said. She handed him a bowl with a small pile of flakes at the bottom.

Cedar raised an eyebrow at his mom. "That's it?"

Tess sighed.

"Why don't you tell them," Tabitha said.

Everyone's heads turned her way in surprise.

"Huh?" Cedar said.

"We could be here for a week, and we might run out of food." She tried to keep the panic out of her voice, but it didn't work.

"Is that true, Mom?" Ashley asked.

Tess narrowed her eyes at Tabitha, as if weighing how much she'd heard and understood of her one-sided conversation. She nodded. "No use hiding the facts from you. We're going to be on strict food rationing until the rain stops and we can head back down the mountain. We don't know how long we might be stuck here."

Cedar groaned. "I'll never make it."

"Yes, you will," Tess said. "It won't be fun, but the whole point of rationing the food is so that we will survive. The good news is that we brought extra fuel, and we can always cook on the woodstove if we run out."

"What will Max eat?" Tabitha asked.

At the sound of his name, Max got up from his seat by the fire and nuzzled Tabitha's hand.

"We'll ration his food too. If he gets hungry enough, he'll probably look for food outside."

"What about us?" Cedar asked. "Can we do the same?"

Tess nodded. "There are still a few huckleberries on the bushes along the path. You can pick some. But don't pick any mushrooms. I don't know them well enough, and we don't have an identification book with us."

They sat and began to eat their meager breakfasts. Tabitha picked at her granola, trying to make it last longer. Cedar gobbled his share in two mouthfuls and went back to bed. Ashley sipped her tea when Tess forced her to. Tess must have eaten earlier, because she had nothing but tea.

After finishing her granola, Tabitha was still hungry. She poured herself another cup of tea to try and fill her stomach, then went and sat by the fire with a musty book she'd found on the shelf. It was a plant identification book. She might as well learn something if they were going to be stuck in the hut for a week.

She flipped through the pages, trying to recognize the different trees, but they all looked the same to her. Maybe if she went outside, she could try to find some of them to identify.

Grabbing her jacket, she went over to the door. "I'm going to take Max for a walk. Maybe I can find us some huckleberries."

Tess raised an eyebrow. "Do you know which ones they are?"

Tabitha waved the plant identification book at her.

"Okay," her aunt said. "There aren't a lot of poisonous berries around here anyway. Stay away from anything white, or anything that looks like a billiard ball, and you'll be fine."

Tabitha put her hand on the door handle.

"And don't take any chances!"

Tabitha slammed the door behind her. Did Tess still think she'd caused Ashley's accident? After their ordeal yesterday, would she take a chance? Get real.

She headed in the opposite direction from the boulders where Ashley had fallen. Max trotted at her heels. She didn't know if she was just getting used to the rain, but it felt like it had eased up ever so slightly. Instead of big drops splashing her face it was more like walking through a mist. Her pace quickened as her mood lifted. Maybe they'd get off the mountain sooner than they thought. Then she slowed.

Maybe the clouds had moved lower, and she was walking inside of one. The mist was actually the cloud hitting her face. Below, the rain was probably still flooding the river.

It still felt good to be outside and away from the hut. She smiled. She was turning into a mountain girl after all. She was the only one of the group who wanted to come back outside after the hike yesterday. That hike was the hardest thing she'd ever had to do, and she'd survived it. Wait till her parents heard. They'd never believe it. Her mom preferred the treadmill to walking outdoors. And most days, the only exercise her dad got was the walk to the bus stop. Her parents created computer programs so complicated that nobody else could understand them, but they didn't have a clue about the wilderness.

Tabitha looked up from her thoughts and realized that she was walking alone. "Max!" she called. No response. "Max!"

All she heard was the rain. He must have run after a squirrel. She continued walking, calling as she went. After she walked for five minutes without seeing him, she decided to turn around. She returned to the spot where she thought she had lost him. In the dense fog, everything looked the same.

"Max, come!" Her voice sounded like her head was covered in a pillow. Maybe Max couldn't even hear her. She stepped a few paces off the trail. Small heather bushes—she recognized them because they grew in her front yard—spotted the ground. She wound around them, calling Max's name. Then she stopped. She could no longer see the path. This was a bad idea. She turned, eyes on the ground to make sure she didn't miss the trail, and walked back down the hill.

The fog made her dizzy. She took a deep breath and kept walking. Within a few seconds, she stepped back onto the trail and sat down to center herself. She needed to think. Searching for Max wouldn't do any good. He could be anywhere. If he chose not to come back to her, there was nothing she could do about it.

Max was a smart dog. He'd come back to the hut when he was ready. But what if he was hurt? She would have to take that chance. If she got lost too, then it would make things worse for everyone.

She began walking back to the hut. As she approached the final bend, she heard a snuffling sound ahead of her. "Max, there you are."

She ran through the fog, ready to give him a hug and a talking-to.

It wasn't Max. She screeched to a stop three feet from a large black bear.

She gasped and froze. She and the bear stared at each other. His huge body blocked the path.

After a moment of the staring contest, he casually turned away from her and started eating berries.

Tabitha's mind swam with images of bear maulings she'd read about in newspapers. Fear coursed through her body, making her tingle. Yet her feet were fixed to the ground. What should she do? The one thing she knew about bears was that you weren't supposed to run. She couldn't saunter past him either.

"I'm going to back up and get out of your way," she said, trying not to sound scared. Her voice shook.

The bear turned to her again. Maybe talking wasn't such a good idea. But she vaguely remembered a talk by a bear expert in grade two. She was pretty sure he'd said to talk so the bear knew you were human.

She edged backward into the fog. As far as she could tell, the bear didn't follow. Berry bushes rustled, but she didn't hear any paws thudding. What to do now that she was out of his sight? She could walk the long way around the lake, but that would take an hour at least. After the big hike the day before, and with so little food in her belly, she didn't think she would have the strength to make it. Besides, Tess would probably start to worry and would come out looking for her when she was halfway around.

She waited a few minutes, but the bear didn't move. The only thing to do was to walk off the path and go around him. Her heart beat so loudly, it drowned out all other sounds as she stepped off the path. It would be so easy to get lost in the fog. She counted her steps, trying to keep in as straight a line as possible. Her feet trampled the heather. If she walked around each bush she'd have no idea which way she was facing.

After twenty steps, she felt far enough from the bear to head back to the path. In the fog he wouldn't see her. Would he smell her? All her senses felt deadened by the fog. Even the inside of her nose was damp. Maybe the bear's would be too. She'd take the risk.

She turned, making sure the downhill slope was on her right. How far to walk? Not far enough, and she'd meet up with the bear again. Too far, and she'd wind up in the creek that ran past the hut.

The terrain became more difficult as she walked. Boulders crept out of the fog and tripped her. Tall bushes covered in red berries blocked her way. She had to weave around them, hoping that she was still heading in the right direction. It felt like the downhill slope was still on her right, but she was so disoriented she couldn't be sure.

Finally she turned again and headed to where she hoped the trail would be. She inched her way toward it, stopping after every step to listen for snuffling and grunting, straining to see a black beast towering over her, ready to charge.

After twenty paces she slowed even more. She must be close to the trail. Twenty-five, twenty-six, twenty-seven. No trail. Maybe she'd taken smaller steps on the way down. At thirty she began to worry. What if she'd walked in the wrong direction while avoiding the bushes? She could be lost out here all night.

She berated herself for not walking the long way around the lake. Because she was too lazy, she might wind up completely lost. First she had lost Max; then she had gotten lost herself. So much for being a mountain girl.

She shook her head. Time to focus. Forty steps. Nothing. Her cheeks prickled with panic. Fifty. Should she call out for help? No. The bear would be the only help that would arrive.

After fifty-eight paces she stepped onto the path. She stopped for a full minute, cocking her head and listening like a chipmunk. No sign of any bear. Cautiously, she crept along the path until she saw the hut. She sprinted the last few steps, flung open the door and slammed it closed behind her.

CHAPTER NINE

"You look like you've seen a ghost," Tess said.

"A bear," Tabitha squeaked. She leaned her back against the door, willing her heart to slow.

Cedar ran to the window. "No way! Where?"

"In the middle of the path." Tabitha's hands shook so much that she could hardly unzip her jacket.

"Cool," Cedar said.

She gave up on her zipper and collapsed onto the bench. "I guess." If you were into a long painful death by dismemberment. She pressed one hand on top of the other to stop the shaking.

"Where's Max?" Ashley mumbled through lips that only opened a crack.

Tabitha froze. She pressed her hands harder into the table. In her panic to get back to the hut, she'd forgotten about Max. "I was going to tell you." Now it would sound like she hadn't cared. "Max took off."

"You left him there?" Ashley's voice grew higher with every word.

"I called and called. I tried searching, but I didn't want to get lost in the fog. I was on my way back to get you guys to help. That's when I ran into the bear."

Tess stirred a package of soup into a pot. "Max is a smart dog. He'll come back."

"What if he chases the bear?" Ashley asked, glaring at Tabitha.

"What if he's hurt?" Cedar asked.

"Let's eat lunch, and then we'll go look for him." Tess put out four bowls of soup with two crackers for everyone but Ashley.

"Lunch?" Cedar asked. "Where's the rest of it?"

"At least you can eat," Ashley said.

Tabitha shivered in her damp clothes. The soup made from a package of dried organic veggie broth tasted delicious, but it didn't fill her up. She thought about Max out there, cowering in the cold. Maybe he'd run off to find food. Maybe he'd had a fight with the bear and lost.

After they'd cleaned out the bowls, Ashley waited until her mom crossed the room and put on her jacket.

Then she leaned close to Tabitha and hissed, "Max better be okay. He was my dad's dog. It'll kill my mom to lose him too."

Tabitha nodded. She dragged herself to the door and reached for her jacket.

Tess put a hand on her arm. "Why don't you stay? You look like another search might do you in."

Tabitha stopped. She didn't feel like going back out and searching anymore, but she didn't want the others to think she didn't care about Max. Ashley and Cedar had their backs to her as they put on their jackets. What did it matter? They would blame her one way or the other.

"Maybe I could take a nap?"

Ashley faced her long enough to roll her eyes, but Tess nodded. "I think that's a good idea. Ashley, you should stay too. You need to conserve your energy."

Ashley didn't respond. She turned her back to her mother and stormed out the door. Tess sighed and followed her.

After the others left, Tabitha climbed up the ladder, pulled on some drier clothes and collapsed on the bunk. Should she have gone to help? She didn't know if she'd be able to sleep, but she'd barely put her head on the pillow before she was out like a light.

Her nap ended with the sound of boots tramping up the outer stairs. She tiptoed to the edge of the sleeping loft. Cedar, Ashley and Tess came in. No Max. She crept back to her bunk before anyone saw her.

"What do we do if Max doesn't come back?" Cedar asked.

"He will," Ashley said.

"But what if he doesn't?" Cedar asked.

Tabitha heard the thud of boots being tossed by the door.

"Let's think positively," Tess said.

"We'll stay here until he does," Ashley said.

"We could run out of food before he gets back," Cedar said.

Tabitha's stomach grumbled. Good point. They wouldn't be able to wait forever.

"Then we'll eat Tabitha," Ashley said.

Tess gasped. "Ashley!"

Tabitha blanched. Obviously her cousin wasn't serious. But how far would she go?

"She lost Max," Ashley said.

"It wasn't her fault," Tess said firmly. "He could have run away from anyone."

"She should have looked harder. It is too her fault."

There was a short silence, followed by a rattle. "Why don't we play Monopoly?" Cedar said.

"Sure."

Tabitha closed her eyes. They were back to their club of two. She never should have tried to be friends with them, or to think that she might be included. Just when things were starting to get better, she had to go and lose Max, who reminded them so much of their dad.

A bench scraped downstairs. "Mind if I play?" Tess asked.

Tabitha could almost hear Ashley's shrug.

Tabitha pulled her sleeping bag over her head. Wasn't that sweet. A family game of Monopoly. She tried to fall back to sleep, but their voices intruded.

Tabitha burrowed deeper into her sleeping bag and put her hands over her ears to block out the voices. What Ashley said was true. Didn't her cousin know how guilty she felt over losing Max? She probably knew Tabitha was eavesdropping.

She'd have to go out and look for Max. But her cousins had just done that. What would be the point? Maybe the fog would lift during the night and she could go look. If she slept in her clothes and put her boots on outside, she could sneak out without waking anyone.

Now that she had a plan, she closed her eyes and her muscles relaxed. She must have fallen asleep, because the next thing she knew it was dark and the others were preparing dinner. She went downstairs.

"Rip Van Winkle's awake," Cedar said.

Ashley glowered. Tabitha ignored her.

Dinner consisted of a small bowl of mushy lentils and more watery soup. Tabitha never knew lentils could taste so good. If Cedar hadn't eaten four brownies on their first night, they might have had something left for dessert.

"D'you think we'll get out of here tomorrow?" Cedar asked as they washed their bowls.

"Not by hiking," Tess said. "That river won't drop until a day or two after the rain stops."

"How else would we get out of here?" Ashley asked.

"They might send a helicopter," Tess said.

"Really?" Tabitha asked. That was the best news she'd heard in days.

Tess nodded. "By now your parents will realize that we didn't make it off the mountain in time. They'll call Search and Rescue."

Tabitha chewed on a fingernail. Would her parents know what to do? They didn't know anything about hiking. "Do they know where we are?"

"I told them before we left," Tess said.

Tabitha frowned. How long would they wait to call Search and Rescue? What if they hadn't written down the name of the mountain?

With these thoughts still swirling in her mind, she began getting ready for bed. Nobody stayed up late. Stomachs growled as they brushed their teeth.

Tabitha was so hungry, even the toothpaste looked good enough to eat.

She had no trouble staying awake in her sleeping bag as her thoughts gnawed at her. After her long sleep during the day, she wasn't ready for an early bedtime. One by one, the others fell asleep. Once she heard them all breathing deeply, she pulled back her sleeping bag, which she'd left unzipped, and crawled out. As she stood up, the room spun around her. She flailed her arm, reaching for the bunk behind her until her vision cleared. She often felt dizzy if she stood up too quickly in the night, but lack of food was making it worse.

Grabbing her jacket, boots and headlamp, she stepped outside in bare feet. She shivered at the feel of the cold, slimy steps. A drizzle of rain splashed her face. On the bottom stair, she put on her boots. Her bare feet chafed against the insides, but it was better than getting another pair of socks wet.

She flicked on the headlamp. The fog had lifted, but the black night pressed in on her. Was she up to this? She didn't know anything about hiking in the dark. She'd stopped looking for Max during the day because she thought she'd get lost. Why did she think she could find him at night?

What about the bear? It must sleep at night. That was one worry she could cross off her list. But what about all the other night critters? She didn't know what nocturnal animals lived in the mountains, but she was sure they would be scary.

Something whizzed by her head. She ducked and swallowed a scream. As she slowly straightened and dared to look around, she saw small objects darting through the night air. Birds? They didn't move like birds.

Bats. Three of them flitted through the sky, like oversized butterflies that had eaten too much sugar. She cringed and pulled her hood tight around her head. Did bats suck your blood, or was that just a nasty fairy tale?

She stepped onto the trail. She'd need to go far enough to call without the others hearing, but not so far that she'd get lost. She crept along, keeping her eyes down so as not to lose the path. The headlamp threw a circle of light in front of her feet. She tried not to think beyond that circle of safety. What lurked outside of it? Maybe hundreds of bats were mounting an attack. She swiveled her head around, shining the light across the bushes that lined the path. Nothing. She shook her head, making the puddle of light wobble. At the rate she was moving, it would take her all night to reach the spot where she'd lost Max.

She lengthened her stride, still focused on the path. Eventually she was far enough from the hut to call.

"Max," she whispered. "Max." Surely the whole mountainside could hear her. She stopped, held her breath and listened. Nothing but silence.

She walked a few more paces and tried again. This time her voice came out as a low murmur. No response. She set her shoulders and breathed deeply, taking in the smell of moist dirt. This wouldn't help Max. She strode along the path, the light bobbling in front of her, then stopped and hollered over and over again, "Max! Maaaax!" She stopped to take a breath. The rain pattered and bats swished, but no dogs barked. It was useless. Max could be anywhere. If she went off the path, she'd get lost. And if Max wanted to come home and wasn't hurt, he'd be back by now.

She turned around to head back to the hut. Her heart felt like a rock sinking to the bottom of the lake. Max would never come back. Ashley and Cedar would hate her forever.

CHAPTER TEN

Small waves from the lake rippled against the shore. Something splashed in the water. Tabitha froze. What was it? She strained to see. There was movement out there. Could it be Max?

She shook her head. Of course not. Why would he be in the lake? But then, stranger things had happened. Whatever was out there made a small noise. Was it a whimper? Maybe Max had swum into the lake to hunt for fish.

"Max!" she called. The animal made the noise again. It definitely sounded like a whimper. He could be hurt. Tabitha began unlacing her boots. She knew the lake would be freezing—after all, it had taken her breath away on a hot sunny day—but she didn't care. If that was Max, she had to save him.

She pulled off her pants and shirt. She'd need something dry to put on when she came out. At least she was the only one out tonight, and no one would see. Holding her breath, she splashed three steps into the water, trying her best to be brave. Her feet went numb almost immediately. Would she be able to swim to Max? She'd have to try.

"What the heck are you doing?" a voice called from behind her.

Tabitha jumped and almost fell in the lake. She spun around and was blinded by a spotlight. She threw an arm in front of her eyes. "Turn that off!"

The spotlight snapped off, and Cedar came into view. Tabitha realized she was standing in her underwear. She crouched, trying to keep her butt out of the water.

"So?" Cedar asked.

"I felt like going for a skinny-dip."

Cedar crossed his arms, reminding Tabitha of Bruce. "Right."

She waved her arm at the island. "I heard something over there, and I think it's Max. I'm rescuing him. If you don't mind, I'll get back to it."

He turned the headlamp back on and pointed it out at the lake. "All I see is a duck. You sure it's worth swimming after in the freezing cold?"

"How do you know it's a duck?"

"I see a long skinny neck and a beak. Don't think Max has either of those."

Tabitha shuffled around, still crouching, and shone her light near Cedar's. She couldn't see anything.

Quack. There was a small splash and then silence.

Tabitha's shoulders drooped. How could she be so dumb? "Can you turn off the light while I get dressed, please?"

Without a word, Cedar did as she asked and turned away from her while she pulled on her shirt and pants.

"Are you totally out of your mind?" he asked, his back still to her.

"What do you care?"

He whipped around to face her. "What do you mean?"

"You and Ashley hate me. Now that I've lost Max, you've both ignored me all day. If I was lost or hurt, the only reason you'd care is because you'd have to spend your precious time looking for me." She pulled on her boots and stomped down the trail. As her headlamp swung past his face, she caught a glimpse of his stunned expression.

He grabbed her arm and spun her around. "I don't blame you for losing Max."

She tried to look into his eyes to see if he was telling the truth, but his headlamp was back on. She pulled her arm out of his grasp. "Why not? I lost him."

Cedar began walking beside her. "It could have happened to anyone. Max has a mind of his own."

"Then why've you ignored me all day?"

He sighed. "I was scared."

"Huh?"

"Max was my dad's dog. It's kinda like losing my dad all over again."

Tabitha couldn't think of anything to say. She nodded in the dark.

"When Dad died, it felt like…like a crevasse opened inside me. You know, like the one he fell into. Except it was a crevasse that opened to all the dark, depressing feelings of the world, and I kept falling into it day after day."

Cedar paused. Tabitha nodded again, hoping he'd go on. "The only way to keep myself on the mountain, out of the crevasse, was to work hard…to do everything he used to do…be strong for Mom and Ashley." He took a deep breath. Tabitha held hers, not wanting to spoil the moment.

"Max started sleeping on my bed after Dad died. Like he knew that I could take his place."

Tabitha shivered. "You don't have to take his place, Cedar. Your mom and Ashley are strong too."

She sensed him pulling at his ponytail. "Maybe I need to do it for me, not them. Anyway, with Max gone, I feel like I'm sliding toward the crevasse again."

They walked a few paces in silence.

"Did you come out here just to look for him?" Cedar asked.

"Yeah."

"Thanks. Even if it was stupid."

"We'd better go in," she replied.

Tabitha didn't bother sneaking around when she entered the hut. If Ashley or Tess woke up, she'd say she'd been at the outhouse. She crawled into her sleeping bag, happy to be cozy and warm.

"Night, Tabitha," Cedar whispered.

"Night." She fell asleep with a smile on her face.

CHAPTER ELEVEN

It felt like only minutes later that she woke to the sound of the door banging open and grunting sounds below. Jumping out of bed, she ran to the ladder, hoping to see Max. Tess beat her there and flew to the first floor.

"Get out of here!" her aunt yelled. "Now!"

A strong smell of wet dog wafted up to the loft. Why would her aunt be chasing Max out? She started to climb down, followed by a groggy Cedar and Ashley.

"Stay up there, it's the bear!"

Tabitha gasped.

"Scram!" Tess was standing in the kitchen, waving her arms at the bear, who was dragging the food bag off the table with his mouth. It eyed her, then stood up on its hind legs and huffed a breath, the bag hanging from its jaws.

"Mom!" Ashley screamed.

"Get going!" Cedar shouted at the bear. He started to climb down the ladder.

"Don't you dare!" Tess called. "The last thing we need is to corner him."

Cedar stopped and climbed back up the top two rungs.

Tess leaped onto a bench, grabbed two pots and started banging them together. Tabitha's mouth hung open. Her aunt never backed off for a second, even as the bear took a step toward her. She growled, shouted, banged her pots and stomped her feet.

The bear huffed again and dropped back to four paws. The wet dog smell mixed with the smell of sweat and fear. Tabitha grabbed Ashley's arm. The three cousins watched in terror as the bear charged at Tess. She flinched but held her ground.

The bear stopped inches from Tess's feet. She continued making her racket. The bear huffed again and reached a paw toward Tess. She jerked her arm back and clanged the pots closer to its face.

At last it turned and ambled out the door, dragging the food bag in its mouth.

Tabitha and her cousins flew down the ladder. Cedar slammed the door shut. Ashley ran to hug her mom while Tabitha hovered behind her.

"Are you okay?" Ashley said.

Tess sank to the bench. Her hands were shaking. "Yeah." She laid one hand over her forearm and pulled away from Ashley. Motioning with her head to the bench, she said, "But he took the food."

Everyone stared at the table where the food bag had once sat. All that was left was a smear of hot chocolate powder that had sprinkled out as the bear shook the bag.

"What do we do now?" Ashley asked.

"We wait, and hope that the helicopter arrives soon," Tess said.

"There are a few berries outside, didn't you say?" Cedar said.

Tabitha stiffened. "We can't go out there—the bear's there."

"I'll need to go eventually," Tess said. "We need water. But you three aren't going anywhere."

"What about the outhouse?" Cedar asked.

Tess grimaced. "Hold it for now. If it gets too bad, you can pee in a pot."

"That's gross," Ashley said.

"I suppose we could go outside in pairs," Tess said.

Neither idea sounded good to Tabitha. "What if the bear's out there waiting for us?"

"I doubt he'll stand around waiting for us to come out. He's got better things to do," Tess said.

"Yeah, like eating our food," Ashley said.

"But how did he get in here in the first place?" Cedar asked.

"The latch must have been open," Tess said. "I could have sworn I closed it last night before going upstairs."

Cedar gave Tabitha a look. Neither one of them said anything. Tabitha decided she'd caused enough problems on this trip already. She wasn't about to take the blame for inviting a bear into the hut. If Cedar wasn't going to speak up, neither would she. She tried to remember which of them had come in last, but couldn't picture it.

"Listen up," Tess said. "We're in for a couple of rough days. We have a bucket of water ready to drink, but we'll need more. I'm going to go out to get some, in case we're all too tired by tomorrow. No matter what happens, I want you guys to keep drinking. Got it?"

Tabitha nodded as Ashley shook her head and said, "Don't go."

Cedar grabbed the water bucket. "I'll do it."

Tess leaped to her feet and blocked his way, still clutching her forearm. "You will not."

"Aw, Mom, you said yourself that he's not going to be waiting for us out there. It's not like it's a grizzly or anything."

"Forget it, Cedar. It broke into the hut and learned it could take our food. I'm not putting you at risk."

"But what about you?"

"I'm the adult here. It's my job."

Cedar stood in front of her, not budging. "You always say that. At least let me come with you."

Tabitha felt the tension rising in Tess. The last thing they needed was a blowout between her aunt and Cedar. Should she interfere? She didn't want to get in the middle of a fight, but she could see Tess's point. She leaned out from the bench and rested a hand on her cousin's arm. "I wish you'd stay here in case the bear comes back."

Cedar frowned at her but relinquished the bucket to Tess.

With a nod to Tabitha, Tess grabbed the bucket and one of the pots from the table and strode to the door.

"Won't it be hard to carry both of those full of water?" Tabitha asked.

Tess shook her head. "I'm not filling up the smaller pot. It's to make noise while I'm outside. I'll bang it against the water bucket." She put them on the floor and rummaged in the first-aid kit.

"What are you doing?" Ashley asked.

"Trying to find the whistle," Tess said. She turned her back to the three kids. "There it is."

Tabitha saw her put something white into her pocket. It looked bigger than a whistle.

Tess faced them again, her hand on the door. "If I'm in trouble, I'll blow the whistle three times. If that happens, bring everything you can find that makes noise and come get me. Otherwise, lock the door and don't even think about leaving. Understand?" She stared directly at Cedar.

All three nodded. Tabitha's heart started pounding again as her aunt opened the door.

"Don't worry," Tess said. "You'll be fine. Remember to lock up." She shut the door and clumped down the stairs.

Cedar hurried to latch the door as Tabitha and Ashley ran to the window.

"I can't believe she's doing this," Cedar grumbled. "Why's she in such a rush?"

Ashley didn't say anything. She pressed her forehead against the window as Tess passed by before turning the corner and heading for the stream.

Tabitha stepped away from the window and sat on the bench. After a few seconds she stood and paced the room.

"Be quiet," Ashley said. "I'm listening."

Tabitha stopped. Silence reverberated off the walls, filling the room with tension. As she listened, small sounds from outside broke through—rain pattering on wet bushes, waves slapping the shore of the lake.

Ashley leaned against the windowsill and buried her head in her arms. "I miss Max."

Cedar nodded. "Me too."

"If Max were here, this would never have happened," Ashley said. "He'd have scared the bear away before it came in."

Or the bear would have eaten him, Tabitha thought. Maybe that had already happened. She closed her eyes and shook her head to clear the image. When she opened her eyes, Ashley and Cedar were staring at each other with drooping faces. Tabitha walked to the kitchen to give them some space. It wasn't just Max they were missing. She couldn't imagine what it would feel like to lose your dad, your dog, and now maybe your mom too.

"I can't believe she'd leave us," Ashley said.

"We need water," Cedar said, sounding as though he were trying to convince himself.

"We'll be okay for a while," Ashley said. "She didn't need to go right away."

Tabitha chewed her lip. Why had Tess left them? She'd been the one to say it wasn't safe in the first place.

And then there was that business with the whistle that didn't look like a whistle. It was as if she was hiding something from them.

At that moment there was a thump on the step. Everyone jumped.

"That was quick," Cedar said, rushing to unlock the door.

"Wait!" Tabitha shouted. "Make sure it's your mom first."

Cedar stopped with his fingers poised above the door handle. "Mom?"

No answer.

The footsteps plodded up two more stairs.

"Mom!" Cedar called. "Is that you?"

Something slapped against the door.

"Maybe it's Max!" Ashley pressed the unhurt side of her face to the glass. She leaped away, one hand covering her mouth. "It's the bear! He's back!"

Heat coursed through Tabitha's body, and every muscle in it tightened into a knot. What if the bear made it through the door? This time Tess wouldn't be here to scare it off.

The bear thumped against the door. The wood shook under the weight.

"I don't know if the latch will hold!" Cedar said.

"What do we do?" Tabitha croaked.

Cedar pushed his back against the door. "Come help me hold it."

Ashley rushed over and stood beside him, holding the door shut. Tabitha took two steps toward them, then stopped. "We need to make noise." She ran to the kitchen and grabbed everything metal she could find—a frying pan, a ladle, a lid and a knife.

Cedar grabbed the ladle and pan. "Good idea."

"What about me?" Ashley asked.

"Bang on the door," Cedar said.

The bear grunted and slapped the handle. Tabitha banged the knife against the pot lid. Ashley hammered on the door. Cedar joined in with the ladle and frying pan. "Go home, bear! Get out of here," he yelled.

The noise was so loud it drowned out all thought. Tabitha watched the door—the only way to tell if the bear was still there. It rattled again. She banged louder. She wished she could cover her ears at the same time as she made the noise.

She thought she'd go crazy with fear waiting for the bear to burst through the door. Her whole being was focused on the door handle and her banging. Sweat dripped into her eyes, but she didn't brush it away. Cedar stopped and motioned for them to do the same. She ignored him. They couldn't stop, or the bear would come in.

Cedar stepped toward her and grabbed her arms, forcing her to stop. She tore her eyes away from the door. The echo of the banging drifted around the room before an eerie silence fell over the hut.

"I think he's gone," Cedar said.

"How do you know?" Tabitha asked. She realized she was panting from the exertion of banging so hard on the pots.

"I haven't felt anything on the door for a while," Cedar said.

Ashley ran to the window again. "I can't see him."

Tabitha sank to the floor and dropped her utensils. She flinched as they clanged.

"Open the door and make sure he's gone," Ashley said.

"Are you crazy?" Cedar yelled.

Footsteps clunked on the stairs. "Oh no, he's back," Tabitha groaned.

Cedar pressed his back against the door. Tabitha stood, but her legs shook so hard she had to steady herself against the wall.

CHAPTER TWELVE

"Open up!"

"It's Mom!" Cedar threw open the door for Tess and grabbed the water bucket from her hand.

"You guys okay?"

"You didn't see it?" Ashley asked.

"What?"

"The bear," Cedar said.

"Not a sign." Tess closed the door, latched it and pulled off her jacket.

"It came back," Tabitha said.

Tess stopped with her hand halfway to the coat hook. "In here?"

"It tried to get in, but we scared it away," Cedar said.

Tess dropped her jacket and pulled Cedar to her in a hug. "What happened? How did you scare it away? Are you guys okay?"

Cedar nodded as Ashley came to join in the hug.

"We're fine. We're good at making noise," Ashley said.

Tabitha shuffled to the kitchen. Tears pricked her eyes. She wanted her mom too. She put the lid and knife on the counter and stood with her shoulders slumped, blinking her eyes to stop the tears.

Tess placed a hand on her shoulder and gently turned her around. "We'll be okay." She wrapped her arms around Tabitha. "You'll see your folks soon."

Tabitha sniffled. But Tess's hug helped. She wiped her tears away. "Thanks."

"Good thing I got the water when I did."

Cedar put the bucket next to the pot that was already full. "We can boil these as we need them."

"Get your water bottles," Tess said. "I want everyone to stay hydrated. With all the excitement this morning, I bet nobody's had anything to drink."

She was right. Now that Tabitha stopped to think about it, she was parched. And starving. And she had to pee. How could you be thirsty and have to pee at the same time? And where was she going to do it? No way she would go to the outhouse with the bear roaming around.

"I need to pee," Ashley said.

Tabitha sighed an inward breath of relief. She wasn't the only one.

"I don't want you heading to the outhouse." Tess picked up one of the pots they'd been banging earlier. "Use this."

"No!" Ashley shouted. "That's disgusting!"

For once, Tabitha agreed with her cousin. She didn't want to pee with everybody watching.

"Then you can go at the bottom of the stairs," Tess said.

Cedar squinted out the window. "No bear. You're safe to go, Ash."

"I have to go too," Tabitha said.

"Safest to go at the same time, while there's no sign of the bear." Tess motioned to the steps with her arm.

Tabitha grimaced. She was supposed to pee right next to Ashley? Her cousin didn't seem bothered by the idea and was already making her way down the steps.

Tabitha took a deep breath and ran out the door. At the bottom of the stairs, she stopped and bent over to peer around the corner of the hut. No bear hiding in the bushes that she could see.

"Quickly, Tabitha!" Tess called.

Tabitha nodded. She turned her back to Ashley and squatted. Nothing happened. She urged herself to go.

Her heart beat so hard she couldn't hear anything else. Maybe the bear was behind her, sizing up her butt, wondering if it would make a tasty snack. She pulled her jacket lower. Ashley finished and walked back up the steps.

"Hurry, Tabitha!" Tess said.

"I'm trying!" She tried to block out the image of Tess and Ashley watching from the steps, and the bear waiting for her around the corner. She started counting slowly. 1, 1, 2, 3, 5, 8, 13. Finally it worked.

When she was done, she jumped up, still pulling up her pants as she moved to the steps.

The rest of the day passed slowly. Tabitha's stomach grumbled, then tightened into a ball of emptiness. Her hunger went beyond feeling hungry, to a feeling of lethargy. All she wanted to do was go back to bed.

Cedar and Ashley bickered the day away. Ashley's whole face was starting to swell and was turning an angry red, matching her mood. Nothing was too small for them to fight about.

"Move over," Ashley said.

Cedar inched his foot away from her and kept reading.

"You didn't even move!"

"Did too. If you've got a problem, go sit on the other bench," Cedar said.

"The light's not as good over there. You move," she said.

Cedar's head stayed buried in his book. "Can't see over there."

Ashley pushed his foot. He pushed back.

Tabitha watched them argue. She had no brother or sister to fight with. At first the bickering was good entertainment. After an hour she was ready to boot them both out the door.

"That's enough," Tess snapped. "If you keep it up, I'll send you both back outside with the bear."

"As if," Ashley said.

"Don't try me," Tess said. "Go sit on the other bench."

Ashley pouted. "Why me?"

"Because you're the one who wanted more room. Move it."

Ashley snatched her book off the bench and stomped to the other side of the picnic table.

Tabitha slouched back in her chair. Now maybe they'd shut up for a few minutes.

Tess picked up her book, then set it on her lap and pressed her hand against her forearm. Tabitha kept an eye on her aunt as she pretended to read. Tess winced. She stood and walked over to the sink. Keeping her back to the kids, she fiddled with something.

Cedar had looked up from his book and was watching Tess as well. "What're you doing, Mom?"

"Just getting some water," Tess called over her shoulder as she reached for her water bottle.

Cedar waited until Tess turned around. "Are you okay?"

Tess smiled. "Of course. Why wouldn't I be?" She gulped water from her bottle. "You should all be drinking more. It's important to keep hydrated, and it'll fill up your stomachs."

Cedar sighed and pushed himself off the bench to get his water bottle. Tabitha took a swig from hers, keeping her eyes on Tess the whole time. But Tess sat as though nothing had happened and went back to reading.

Tabitha thought the day would never end. By five o'clock the hut was dark. With no dinner to prepare, the hours until bed stretched before them. She was sick of reading about flowers. She craved a huge bowl of spaghetti and meatballs. Or a juicy McDonald's hamburger. She could probably eat five of them. Finally, at eight o'clock, she gave up. "I'm going to bed."

Tess nodded. "Good idea."

"Should we put a chair or something against the door?" Tabitha asked.

Tess thought for a moment. "Wouldn't hurt," she said.

Tabitha dragged her chair to the door and tilted it, lodging the chair back under the handle. It wouldn't keep an angry bear out, but it made her feel more secure.

Hauling herself up the ladder was a huge effort. She couldn't believe how much weaker she felt after a day of not eating. At this rate she wouldn't be able to get out of bed the next day. No wonder Ashley was so grumpy. She'd had another whole day of not eating, on top of dealing with the pain in her face.

The other three followed shortly after. Tabitha lay in bed and listened to the rustle of everybody getting ready for sleep. After lying around feeling listless all day, her body was now fully awake. Her stomach churned with hunger and her mind whirled with worries.

She thought of kids across the world who went through most of their lives with empty stomachs. Surely she could make it a night or two. But what if the rescue didn't come? What if her parents had given Search and Rescue the name of the wrong mountain peak, and they'd tried a rescue, found no one, and now thought they were all dead? She shook her head, trying to clear the bad thoughts. Her parents might be so focused on their computer programming that they sometimes forgot about dinner, but they weren't dumb. They'd remember the name of a mountain, wouldn't they?

She woke at dawn with a gnawing pain in her stomach and guzzled some water to try and fill it up. It helped, but she knew she wouldn't be able to trick her body for long.

She sat up and stretched. Everyone else was still asleep. It surprised her to see Tess still in bed. Her aunt had been up before anyone else every other day of the trip. Tabitha lay down and tried to fall back to sleep. No sense getting up with nowhere to go, nothing to do and nothing to eat.

After about ten minutes, Tess stirred in her sleeping bag. Tabitha rolled over, waiting until her aunt was fully awake before she spoke. Tabitha watched Tess push herself to a seated position and look out the window.

Then she pulled the sleeve of her shirt back and peered at her arm.

Tabitha watched silently, puzzled as her aunt poked at her arm. It was hard to see in the dim light, but it looked as though she had another shirt on underneath, something white and brown.

Tess swung her legs off the bunk, giving Tabitha a clear view of her arm. Tabitha sucked in her breath. It wasn't a shirt, it was a bandage. A white bandage with blotches of dried blood on it.

CHAPTER THIRTEEN

Tabitha thought about what her aunt had done the day before. Everything clicked into place. Tess had rushed out to get water so she could bandage her arm. And that's why she'd been holding it all day. But how had she cut it? Tabitha remembered the bear coming close to Tess. Had it grazed her arm? She hadn't screamed, but she had jerked her arm back.

Tabitha pushed herself up in bed and whispered, "Is it bleeding?"

Tess gasped and pulled her sleeve over the wound. "I didn't know anyone else was up."

"You don't have to hide it," Tabitha said. "Was it the bear?"

Tess nodded. "It's okay. It only scratched me."

"It's a bear, not a cat!"

Tess shrugged. "I was so worked up about getting it out of here, I honestly didn't notice that much at the time. But now it's infected."

"Why didn't you tell us?" Tabitha asked.

"I didn't want you to worry."

Tabitha sighed. Wouldn't her aunt ever learn that they'd find things out anyway? She was so busy protecting them that she made life harder for everyone. "If you'd told us, we could have helped you take care of it better."

Tess closed her eyes. "Maybe. It's easy to forget that you three are tougher than you look."

Cedar rolled over and hung off his bunk. "What's going on?"

Tess stared hard at Tabitha, who ignored her. "Your mom's hurt," Tabitha said.

Cedar hopped across the floor in his sleeping bag. "What happened?"

Tess held out a hand to stop him. "Relax. I cut my arm yesterday. It's a little infected, but nothing serious."

"Don't you have antibiotic ointment?" Cedar asked.

"Mmm-hmm," Tess said. She walked over to where Ashley still slept and bent over her face.

"You didn't use it, did you?" Cedar hopped behind her, still holding his sleeping bag around his chest.

"I'm worried Ashley will get an infection," Tess said.

"But you're no help to us if *you* get sick from an infection!" Cedar said.

Tess waved him away. "I'll be fine." She turned her back to him and went downstairs, using her right arm to balance herself on the way down.

Ashley rolled over in her sleeping bag. "What's going on?" she asked groggily. Her cheek was blue. One eye was barely visible due to the swelling around it. The other was sunk deep into the socket. She looked like she was dressed as a zombie for Halloween.

"Mom's—," Cedar started to say, but Ashley rolled over and fell back asleep.

Tabitha chewed her lip. Ashley usually had so much energy. This didn't seem like her. She climbed down the ladder. "Tess, I think you'd better come upstairs."

Tess was sitting at the table, dabbing at her arm with a web of cotton dressing. A long cut, crusted with blood, split her red, swollen arm.

Tabitha gagged at the sight of it.

Tess started to wrap a fresh bandage around her arm. "I'll be right up as soon as I'm done." She motioned to her first-aid kit with her head. "Bring this up for me."

Tabitha nodded and followed Tess as she pulled herself up the ladder, swinging back and lunging up with her good arm at each rung. Halfway up, she rested, her good arm hooked over a rung. After a few deep breaths, she grunted and continued. At the top, she pulled herself into the loft and hurried to Ashley's side, pushing Cedar away from his spot beside Ashley's head.

"What's going on?" she asked.

"Ashley won't stay awake," Cedar said.

Tess squeezed the skin on the back of Ashley's hand and pressed a finger onto her forearm. They'd gotten stuck on the mountain, attacked by a bear and run out of food, yet Tess had never looked truly worried. Now her face was pinched and her head drooped. Tabitha's stomach twisted in a knot. Was Ashley going to die?

Tabitha reached behind her for her bunk and fell onto it. As much as her cousin drove her crazy, she didn't want her to die. She was only thirteen. It wasn't fair. She should be downstairs, grumping at Tabitha and bickering with Cedar.

Tess's voice broke into her thoughts. "She's severely dehydrated. Cedar, go get us some water."

Cedar didn't move. He had shuffled around to the head of the bunk and was stroking Ashley's hair, his face knotted with worry.

"I can do it," Tabitha said. She hurried down the ladder, filled Ashley's water bottle and brought it back to Tess.

Tess held it to Ashley's lips, but she batted it away.

Cedar pulled Ashley to a half-seated position. "Drink."

This time, when Tess held up the water, Ashley took a few small sips. Her lips couldn't close over the bottle's mouth, and water spilled down her chin.

"Good girl," Tess said. "Let's try some more."

After another few mouthfuls, Ashley pushed the bottle away and refused to take any more.

Tess sat back on her heels. "We'll try again later."

Cedar eased Ashley back onto her bed, and she rolled over to face the wall. Tess went down the ladder. Tabitha followed, leaving Cedar sitting on his sister's bed.

Tess paced around the hut, cradling her arm. Tabitha sat on a chair by the stove, trying to stay invisible.

"No food, no medicine," her aunt muttered. "How much longer do you think we'll last?"

Tabitha was pretty sure Tess wasn't talking to her.

"Yeah, I'm worried too."

Tabitha's eyes drifted to the box containing her uncle's ashes. They really needed to scatter them.

"I'll be fine, as long as we get out of here soon."

Cedar slid down the ladder. Tess stopped pacing.

"She's asleep," he said.

Tess nodded and sagged onto the bench. After a few minutes of silence she stood again. "I'm going back to bed too. No sense wasting energy."

As if they needed reminding. Tabitha nodded. She'd love to curl up with Max by the fire right now. With all the excitement, she'd forgotten about him. She wondered what he was doing out there. Had he managed to avoid the bear?

She dozed off in her chair and fell into a nightmare. She was chasing Max up a mountain. Every time she caught up to him, a bear jumped out of a bush, swiped her arm and left bloody gashes across it. They healed when Cedar swabbed them with antibiotic ointment, but only long enough for her to chase Max to the next bush and the next bear.

"Max!" a voice called. She jerked upright, swiveled her head around to see who had shouted. Was it her? Cedar was stretched out on the bench, asleep.

"No! Max!" It was Ashley.

Shaking off the fog of sleep, Tabitha hauled herself up the ladder to Ashley's bed. Her cousin was rolling back and forth on her bunk, her puffy face distorted with fear.

"No," she moaned.

Tabitha stood over her. Were you supposed to wake someone in a nightmare? Or let her sleep? She needed to sleep. But it seemed cruel to leave her in her dream.

She stroked Ashley's arm. "It's a dream, Ashley. Wake up."

Ashley kept moaning and thrashing.

Tabitha grabbed her harder. "Ashley! Wake up!"

Ashley's eyes flew open. She jerked her arm away from Tabitha. A look of pure hatred crossed her face. "You! You lost him. You killed him."

Tabitha stepped back from Ashley. Did her cousin really hate her that much?

"You were dreaming, Ash," Cedar said from behind her.

Tabitha swung around. How had he gotten there?

For a moment, Ashley's face softened. "You mean Max is back?"

"No. But that doesn't mean he's dead."

Ashley's face darkened again. "It's her fault. Get her out of here."

Tabitha pushed past Cedar, not wanting to see the look on Ashley's face anymore. She slouched on the bench downstairs, watching the rain, wondering if she'd be stuck here until she died of starvation, or if Ashley would kill her first.

Cedar came down a few minutes later. "I'm worried about her."

Tabitha nodded.

"I think the pain's making her say things she doesn't mean."

"She's saying exactly what she means," Tabitha said.

Cedar tugged at his ponytail. "My mom must be really tired if she didn't wake up through any of that."

Tabitha nodded. "Do you think it's because of her arm?"

"Maybe." He walked to the window and stared out, as if willing the helicopter to arrive.

CHAPTER FOURTEEN

Tabitha took up her spot by the woodstove. She shivered. The fire had gone out earlier that morning, and no one had thought to restart it. The room had grown cooler as the afternoon passed. She stood and looked for firewood. "Hey, Cedar, wasn't there a pile of wood here?"

"To the right of the stove," Cedar said without turning around. "In the wooden box."

The box had a few small scraps of wood and bark lying in the bottom. "I think we have a problem."

Cedar turned. "What now?"

"We're out of wood."

"So?"

"Can't you tell how cold it is? Don't you think we should keep Ashley and your mom warm at least?"

Cedar's head drooped. Then he stood straight again. "You're right. Let's go get some wood."

"Us?"

"Who else?"

Tabitha swallowed. Of course. The wood wouldn't fly in the door. If only they had a magic wand. She'd give anything to be Hermione Granger right now. "Let's go."

Cedar took the whistle and the wood carrier. Tabitha grabbed a pot and lid. They checked through the window, then opened the door a crack. Listened. No snuffs, snorts, or sounds of small animals being consumed. They crept outside.

Tabitha let Cedar check around the corner. They both rushed along the side of the building to the woodpile under the eave. Cedar dropped the wood bag on the ground and tossed logs onto it. Tabitha scanned the area behind them, not wanting to be caught by surprise.

Cedar stopped. Tabitha turned, expecting him to pick up the full bag. He stood with his arms braced against the pile, the half-full bag at his feet.

"What's wrong?" she asked in alarm.

Cedar didn't answer. His shoulders shook.

Tabitha's mouth fell open. Cedar was crying? A sob escaped and echoed off the wall of the hut.

Tabitha really, really wanted to get back into the hut. But it would be cruel to make Cedar hurry when he was so upset. She peered into the fog. Nothing moved. She stepped closer to Cedar and touched him on the shoulder. "Do you want to talk about it?"

He shook his head. Tears dripped down his cheeks.

Tabitha stepped away. Her ears reached into the fog, listening for sounds of the bear.

After a few minutes, he stood and wiped his arm across his cheeks. "What'll I do if I lose Mom? And Ash?"

Tabitha sucked in her breath. How could she answer that? You didn't say *Oh, it'll be okay* to someone who had already lost his dad. They both knew it probably wouldn't be okay, unless help came soon.

"We have to get off the mountain," she said.

Cedar slumped further. "We can't."

"Maybe the river's lower," Tabitha said.

He spun to face her. "It's still raining. Even if it stopped, we can't leave Mom and Ashley like this. And it wouldn't be safe for one of us to go alone."

Tabitha dropped her chin onto her chest. He was right. It wouldn't solve anything. But she hated being stuck here, waiting. It felt like they were under siege.

A twig snapped. Tabitha jumped. "Let's get out of here!"

Cedar tossed a few more logs into the bag and lifted the handles. Tabitha scurried to the corner of the hut. She checked to make sure all was clear, then ran up the stairs. Cedar bumped up behind her.

He dropped the bag by the fire, and they both ran to the window. A robin flew past and settled on a tree.

Tabitha giggled. "Is that what spooked us?"

Cedar barked out a laugh. "Probably."

Something untwisted in Tabitha's stomach. They were safe this time. Her giggle turned into a laugh. She met Cedar's eyes.

"We're all going mental," he said.

"Yup." Tabitha laughed harder. Cedar started too. It felt so good to laugh that Tabitha didn't even try to stop. Before long they were both crouched on the floor, holding their stomachs, unable to control themselves.

"This is crazy." The words squeaked out of Cedar's mouth.

"I know," Tabitha gasped.

They both collapsed in another fit of laughing. Tabitha never wanted it to stop, no matter how much her stomach hurt.

"Cedar!" Ashley called from upstairs.

Abruptly, Cedar's face fell serious again. He leaped to his feet, leaving Tabitha in a stunned puddle on the floor.

He ran to the ladder. "Yeah?"

"Water," Ashley croaked.

Cedar ran up and came back a few minutes later with the water bottle, a crease of worry between his brows.

"She doesn't look good. And Mom's still sleeping."

Tabitha sighed. It had felt nice to forget for a few minutes. She pushed herself to her feet. As she stood, the room grew black around her. She reached out, trying to find something for balance, and fell onto the bench. After a few moments, the blackness cleared. Cedar was staring at her with panic in his eyes.

"What happened?"

She waved him away. "It's not a big deal. I stood up too fast."

He shoved her water bottle across the table. "You better drink some more too."

She nodded and took a sip as he climbed the ladder. She'd never had a blackout in the middle of the day.

Her stomach grumbled so loudly, she was surprised no one came looking for the bear.

Ashley and Cedar were murmuring upstairs. Then she heard, "Stay away from her. She's the enemy!"

Tabitha shrank onto the bench. She wasn't sure which was worse: the things her cousin was saying, or the fact that she must be really going downhill if she was saying them out loud. At least before, she'd been sneaky about making Tabitha feel bad.

She sat with her arms wrapped around her legs and listened to Cedar calm his sister. It began to grow dark outside, and things grew quiet upstairs. She shivered. Cedar didn't seem to be in a rush to come back. She eyed the fireplace. She might as well try and build a fire herself. It was too early to go to bed—she'd toss and turn all night. Besides, the last thing she wanted was for Ashley to see her.

She swung open the door to the woodstove. Taking three pieces of newspaper from the stack beside the stove, she crumpled them and placed them on the grate. It took her three tries to make a teepee of kindling that stood on its own. Then she laid a larger piece of wood, one she hoped was dry, across it all, balancing it on the grate so it wouldn't collapse her teepee.

She pulled the matches from their perch on the ledge above the woodstove and removed one from the box. She hated lighting matches. If she held them too close to the head, she worried her fingers would get singed when they lit. So she held them farther out, and half the time the match broke.

Taking a deep breath, she struck the match. Nothing. She struck again. It lit. Carefully she brought it to the fire and touched it against the paper. Not wanting to take any chances, she held it to five different spots of paper, dropping it into the flames just before it burned her finger.

She sat back on her heels and watched, praying that it would catch and she wouldn't have to start the process all over again. The paper caught quickly, flames licking the top of the stove. After a few moments the paper burned up and the flames died. She'd failed. What did she think, that she was some kind of mountain woman?

But then she heard a crackling. A piece of kindling in the back was burning. She sat forward and blew softly, the way she'd seen Cedar do. The flames grew higher, and another piece caught. Before long all three pieces were burning nicely, and the bigger piece was starting to catch too.

"Did you do that?"

Tabitha fell onto her butt, startled at the sound of Cedar's voice. "Yeah."

"Wow. I didn't think you had it in you."

Tabitha grinned. Then frowned. Did he think she was completely useless?

He waved his hands in front of himself. "I didn't mean it like that. Just that I didn't know you could build a fire."

"Neither did I." She stood and stepped away from the stove. This camping stuff wasn't so hard after all. If you didn't mind starvation, wild animal attacks, dehydration and infections that might kill your companions.

CHAPTER FIFTEEN

She and Cedar sat on the floor in front of the fire in comfortable silence. The smell of wood smoke filled the air. As her fire grew stronger, some of the cold seeped from Tabitha's body, although her backside still felt icy.

"I'm sorry about Ashley," Cedar said.

"Me too," Tabitha said. "I hope she'll be okay."

"I mean about what she said to you."

Tabitha shrugged. "At least she's saying it out loud."

"She doesn't mean it," Cedar said.

"I think maybe in her heart she does."

Cedar shook his head. "She's been really messed up since Dad died. It's like this has put her over the edge."

Tabitha nodded, wondering how Cedar could be so calm. Was he letting this flow off him the way he did with the bullies at school? Was that possible?

He stood and threw another log on the fire, then paced around the room.

Maybe he wasn't as calm as he seemed.

"I'm going to bed," Cedar said. "I want this day to be over."

Tabitha stood slowly, not wanting to black out again. "I can't believe it, but I'm actually tired."

"Yeah." Cedar closed the doors on the woodstove to make the fire last longer. "Not eating for days does that to you, I guess."

Tabitha's arms were barely strong enough to pull her up the ladder. She stopped with her eyes peeking across the floor and checked to see that Ashley was sleeping before she crept to her bed.

Cedar leaned over his mom. He pulled back the sleeve of her shirt. "Come look at this," he whispered.

Tabitha tiptoed to Tess's bunk. "What?"

Cedar pointed to Tess's arm. A red line snaked from her bandage up toward her arm. "That wasn't there this morning."

"You're right," Tabitha said. "What is it?"

"I think it's the infection she was worried Ashley would get."

"What do we do?"

"Get that tube of ointment." Cedar began unwrapping the bandage.

Tess woke. "What're you doing?" she asked groggily.

"Taking care of your arm," Cedar said.

Tabitha grabbed the first-aid kit from the end of Tess's bunk and rummaged through it until she found the ointment. She handed it to Cedar, who squeezed a line of it onto Tess's arm. The cut was definitely infected. Yellow pus glistened along the scab. Tabitha could almost see the puffy skin throbbing.

"Thank you," Tess murmured, and closed her eyes.

Cedar wrapped a fresh bandage around her arm and laid it at her side. He rested his forehead on her mattress.

Tabitha put a hand on his shoulder. "Let's get some sleep."

Cedar pushed himself up. "Yeah."

Tabitha slept fitfully. Both Tess and Ashley called out during the night. Each time, she woke with her heart pounding and needed to repeat the Fibonacci string to fall back asleep. In the early morning she woke again and lay there listening, trying to figure out what had woken her. Her aunt and Ashley were both quiet. Cedar was breathing deeply.

Then it hit her. The silence had woken her. The rain had stopped. She'd gotten used to the clatter on the roof. Now that it had stopped, the silence rang in her ears. She pressed her face to the window. The sky was brightening, and it appeared that even the fog was lifting.

She crept downstairs.

Her fire had gone out overnight. She decided not to light one right away because the sound might wake the other three. She sat shivering on the bench, her body achy and tired, dreaming of the breakfast she would have when she got home. Pancakes dripping with maple syrup and butter, with blueberries, strawberries and raspberries. And French toast. And maybe an egg on the side. Make that two. If they got home.

Her head jerked up as she realized a noise outside had encroached on her daydream. A low roar. Oh no. The bear was back. The roar grew louder. She relaxed as she realized it was only a helicopter.

A helicopter! She ran to the window. It was coming toward the lake. Their rescue! If it knew they were here. "Wake up! The helicopter's coming!" she shouted.

She ran out the door in her bare feet and flew down the stairs. The black closed in around her, and she thought she might faint. She flailed her arms, grasping for the handrail, and waited impatiently for the feeling to pass. The world cleared. She took a deep breath and jogged, slower this time, out to the lake. As the helicopter grew closer, she waved her arms frantically.

Would they see her? She felt so small against the back-drop of trees and mountains.

What could she do to make them see? She yanked off her fleece and waved it in the air. The helicopter wiggled and flew to the other end of the lake. Her shoulders drooped as it flew away. It hadn't seen her. They'd be stuck here forever.

But then it changed direction again and came lower. She realized it was heading for a clearing to the left of the hut. They were being rescued!

She turned to run back to the hut. After a few steps she slowed to a fast walk. Cedar was downstairs, yanking on his boots.

"It's landing!" she called.

He nodded. "I'll go tell them we need help. You get Ashley and my mom up."

Tabitha climbed the ladder. She ran to Tess and shook her shoulder. "Wake up! The helicopter's here!"

Tess's eyes cracked open. "What?"

"We're being rescued. You have to get up!"

Recognition slowly dawned in Tess's eyes. She pushed herself to a seated position. That was as far as she got.

"C'mon, Tess, you can do it."

Tess nodded. "I just need a rest."

Tabitha unzipped her aunt's sleeping bag. "You can rest once we're out of here. We need to get going."

She pulled Tess's legs and placed them on the floor. "If we don't get out of here soon and get you and Ashley to a hospital, one of you might die!"

Tess's head snapped up. She looked over at Ashley, and her mouth formed an *O*. She pushed herself out of bed with her good arm and started to walk toward her.

"Cedar's gone to get the pilot. We'll get Ashley next. You need to go down the ladder."

Tess nodded and wobbled toward it.

Tabitha got there first. "I'll help you from below. Can you use your good arm?"

"I think so."

Tabitha breathed a sigh of relief that her aunt was talking. Things would be okay. She climbed halfway down the ladder and braced herself. Tess knelt, then flattened onto her stomach and dropped her legs over the edge. Tabitha helped guide them to the rung. As her aunt put her weight on them and reached for the first rung with her hand, Tabitha pushed against her back with one hand to support her weight. They worked their way down the ladder, one rung at a time, until Tess reached the bottom.

Tabitha helped her put on her shoes, then opened the door. "Can you get to the helicopter by yourself?"

"Where is it?"

"About a minute's walk to the clearing."

Tess nodded. As Tabitha opened the door, Cedar came up the stairs with the pilot.

"I'm Pete," he said. "We're extracting people up and down the valley. We don't have time to linger, so leave your stuff. You can come back for it later."

Fat chance of that, thought Tabitha. She'd never be coming back to this place, stuff or no stuff.

"Cedar, help your mom," Tabitha said. "I'll get Ashley."

Cedar nodded and hooked Tess's arm around his shoulder. The pilot came into the hut.

"You need me?" he asked Tabitha.

"Yeah. This could be tough." She faced the ladder one last time. Each trip up took more and more effort. "You have any food?"

"I've got some caramels in the helicopter."

Tabitha started salivating at the word *caramel*. Even the idea of it gave her the strength to climb the ladder.

Ashley lay motionless on her bunk. Tabitha nudged her shoulder. "Hey, Ashley. We're being rescued. Time to go."

Ashley opened her eyes and stared blankly at Tabitha. Then her eyes focused on Tabitha's face, and she drew back.

Pete stepped forward. "Miss, we're taking you to a hospital."

Ashley's face darkened. "Is Max back?"

Tabitha sighed. "No."

"I'm not leaving without Max."

"Ashley, you're sick. You need to leave now, Max or no Max." Tabitha reached a hand to help Ashley to sit up.

Ashley hit her arm out of the way. "Don't touch me! I'm not going!"

"You have to come!" Tabitha insisted. "If you stay here, you'll die."

Ashley crossed her arms and glowered at them.

Tabitha sized up the pilot. His arm muscles bulged through his T-shirt. "We have to get her out of here," she said.

He nodded and moved to the head of the bed. Tabitha stood by her feet.

"On three," Pete said.

"What're you doing?" Ashley asked.

Tabitha ignored her. "One, two, three!" She wrapped her arms around Ashley's knees while the pilot scooped her up under her arms. They lifted her off the bed and took a step into the middle of the room.

Ashley began thrashing. "Put me down! Let go!"

Tabitha couldn't believe how much strength Ashley had for someone so sick. One foot got loose and kicked her in the chest, but Tabitha wrapped her arms around again and held on as tightly as she could. As much as she'd like to let her cousin drop and leave her to fend for herself, she knew she had to get her to safety.

"How are we going to get down the ladder?" Tabitha asked.

"I'll help!" Cedar called from downstairs. His face appeared at the top of the ladder. "What's going on?"

"Try and talk to her," Tabitha said. "She won't come without Max."

But there was no talking to Ashley. She'd worked herself into a fit and wouldn't stop thrashing long enough to recognize that Cedar was there.

"Quick," said Pete. "I don't know how much longer I can hold her!"

"Lower her as far as you can, and we'll catch her at the bottom." Cedar dropped back to the ground floor.

Pete raised his eyebrows. "You sure? If we drop her, it could damage her face even more."

"You have a better idea?" Cedar called from below.

Pete and Tabitha shook their heads.

Pete held Ashley under her armpits while Tabitha climbed halfway down the ladder, ducking to avoid her cousin's thrashing feet.

"Don't miss!" Cedar called.

"I'm going to lean over as far as I can," Pete said. "She won't have far to go." He dangled Ashley's feet over the edge.

When her hips were over, she started screaming even louder. "Let me go! I'm staying here!"

Cedar reached up and grabbed her legs. "Now!"

Pete let go and Ashley fell into their arms, a kicking, screaming mess. The effort knocked Tabitha to the floor. But they had managed to cushion Ashley's fall. Pete climbed down the ladder to help Cedar try to control her, while Tabitha scrambled up from the floor and ran to get the door.

Pete threw Ashley over his back in a fireman's hold and jogged to the helicopter. Tabitha hurried after him, the thought of the promised caramels giving her the energy to move quickly.

CHAPTER SIXTEEN

The helicopter door stood open. Pete climbed up the steps and dropped Ashley inside. Coming after him, Tabitha saw that he'd managed to strap Ashley into her seat. Tess sat beside her, trying to calm her.

"It'll be okay," Tess said.

Ashley sobbed and sobbed, but no tears fell from her eyes. "I don't want to leave him!"

Tabitha stood for a moment on the threshold of the helicopter. The only two seats left were the one next to Ashley and the passenger seat. She crawled through to the front. Cedar climbed in beside Ashley. Pete was checking the controls.

"Pete," she said. "Could we have those caramels now?"

"Right, I forgot." He passed a bag to her. She forced herself to only keep two for herself before passing the bag back. She unwrapped one and popped it into her mouth. The sweet, buttery flavor coated her tongue. All too soon, it was over. She ate the second one. Her stomach still felt empty. She'd need to eat the whole bag to satisfy her hunger.

Pete picked up the radio and began talking. "Pete to base station. Please connect me with Squamish hospital."

Tess gasped. Tabitha spun around. "What's wrong?"

"The ashes!" She tried to undo her seatbelt, but couldn't lift her arm to do it.

"Mom, stop!" Cedar yelled. "I'll go get them!"

Tabitha opened her door. "No, I will. You look after those two."

"Hey!" called Pete. Tabitha ignored him and ran stumbling back to the hut. She couldn't believe how out of breath she was from the short run. Up the steps one more time. Into the hut. The ashes sat in their usual place on the shelf.

"Hi, Bruce," she breathed. "Looks like you're going back home again. I think you'd be happier up here, but I'm not arguing with Tess." She screwed up her face and grabbed them off the shelf.

"Wow, Bruce. You weigh a lot." Running with the heavy box in her hand was awkward. She settled into a fast walk.

"C'mon," Pete called from the helicopter. "We need to get moving."

Tabitha climbed the steps to the helicopter once again, and passed the ashes to Tess.

"Thanks," her aunt said. A tear trickled out of her eye as she stroked the box.

The rotors began to spin and roar. Pete checked to make sure they had their straps fastened, and a moment later they were lifting off the ground. Tabitha's stomach lurched. In all the ruckus of getting Ashley out of the hut, she'd forgotten to be excited about her first helicopter ride. She pressed her face against the window and watched the ground drop away beneath her. Soon the whole lake was visible. As they made a sharp turn to head for the Squamish Valley, she caught a glimpse of something yellow moving along the trail. She did a double take. Could it be?

She glanced behind her to see if anyone else had noticed, but Cedar and Tess were both gripping Ashley's hands and talking to her. When she looked out the window again, Max, if it was really him, had disappeared. Had she imagined the whole thing? Maybe she was hallucinating. It would be possible, after everything they'd gone through in the last three days. She shook her head. But wait, there it was again. A yellow spot moving on the path.

Tabitha sucked in her breath. Max was alive. And they were leaving him behind.

The helicopter made a sharp turn to the right. The path—and Max—were no longer visible. She sat back in her seat. Max was really there. She had to come back to get him.

Before she knew it, they were landing at the Squamish hospital. As soon as they touched down, four attendants dressed in pale blue scrubs ran to the helicopter, hunched over to avoid the rotors. Each pushed a wheelchair.

"I can walk," Tabitha said.

"We'd still like you to ride in this," said a nurse wearing a nametag that said *Patricia*. Tabitha sighed and sat. It did feel good to have someone push her around.

As Patricia wheeled her into the building, she saw two familiar figures standing by the door. "Mom! Dad!" She leaped to her feet and ran the rest of the way.

"Tabitha!' her mom cried as she wrapped her in a hug. The tears that Tabitha had fought to contain over the last few days spilled out as she allowed herself to be engulfed in her parents' arms.

After a few minutes Patricia gently tugged at her arm. "Tabitha, we'd like to check you out in triage."

"I'm fine, really," Tabitha said. "Just hungry."

"We'll get you some food as soon as we've made sure you're okay."

Tabitha sighed and sat back in the wheelchair. Her parents followed closely behind. Tabitha grinned. Were they worried that if they let her out of her sight they wouldn't see her for another seven days?

She let the nurse take her temperature and blood pressure, and ask her several questions before saying, "Can I have the food now?"

"Yes," Patricia said. "You're fine. Eat, and then we'll release you. And remember to drink lots of water."

Tabitha's eyes widened at the feast Patricia wheeled in front of her. Chicken, rice, tomato soup, Jello and a fruit cup. She cut into the chicken, too hungry to enjoy the taste, barely swallowing before she shoveled the next chunk in. Within minutes the whole tray was empty.

"That was impressive," her dad said.

"Any more?" Tabitha asked.

"You shouldn't overdo it," her mom said. "I'll make you something at home after we check on Tess and Ashley."

Tabitha pushed herself out of the wheelchair. With a wave to Patricia, they walked out the door.

They found Cedar pacing the reception area. Tabitha's mom and dad gave him a hug, but he stared down the hallway, barely seeming to register their arms around him.

"Did you eat?" Tabitha asked.

Cedar nodded. "Two trays."

"Where are your mom and Ashley?"

"They've both been admitted. They're in a room down that hallway, but I'm not allowed in until the doctor's done." He gripped the back of a chair. "This is harder than anything we did up there."

Tabitha reached up and pulled lightly on his ponytail. "They'll be okay. We're in the hospital now, and they'll get the medicine they need."

Cedar tore his eyes off the hallway and smiled at Tabitha. "I hope you're right."

Tabitha thought about seeing Max from the helicopter. Should she tell him? No. He didn't need to worry about anything else.

A young woman with a stethoscope draped around her neck approached their group.

"You can go in now, Cedar."

"How are they?" Tabitha's mom asked.

"They're both asleep. Tess is hooked up to iv antibiotics. I can't say for sure, but I think we've caught the infection early enough. She should be fine."

"And Ashley?" Cedar asked.

"We've pumped her full of fluids. There's no more worry about dehydration. We ran some X-rays on her cheek. The bone is broken, but I don't think surgery will be necessary. She'll be sore for a few weeks though."

Everybody breathed out in unison. Cedar ran to the door with a quick wave.

"I'd like to see my sister," Tabitha's mom said.

Tabitha put a hand on her arm. "Why don't you come back later? Cedar needs some time alone with her."

Her mom's eyes opened wide. Then she nodded.

"Let's go home," her dad said.

CHAPTER SEVENTEEN

When they arrived home, Tabitha ran to the bathroom. She was so happy to see the toilet, she almost hugged it. She showered, reveling in the beautiful hot water coursing over her, washing away seven days of muck, fear and anxiety.

She meant to eat another meal, but her bed called out to her and drew her in. She lay on the soft mattress and for a moment did nothing but enjoy the clean, slippery sheets beneath her legs. Then she sighed. Max was still up on the mountain. She had to go back.

Her heart jumped. Back across the river. Up the treacherous muddy trail to face the bear. How would she find Max when she got to the hut? She couldn't do it alone.

She woke to her mother gently shaking her and a familiar rumbling in her stomach.

"Time for breakfast," her mom said.

"But it's the afternoon."

Her mom smiled. "You slept all night."

Tabitha sat up and rubbed her eyes, then threw on some clothes and padded into the kitchen. Her dad was buried in a programming magazine. Some things never changed. And that was okay with her.

"Have you heard from the hospital?" She filled a huge bowl with corn flakes and loaded a spoonful of brown sugar on top.

Her mom nodded. "I spent most of the night there. Tess and Ashley are both stable. They'll probably be discharged in a day or two." Tabitha chewed her cereal, filled with relief at the news. She wondered if Ashley would feel the same way if the tables were turned. Could her cousin hate her that much? If she brought Max back, maybe Ashley wouldn't hate her anymore.

She spent the day lying around on the couch, resting, enjoying the small pleasures in taking food out of the fridge and turning on a tap to get water. She tried hard not to think about Max and Ashley.

◎

Her mom woke her again the next morning. "Bus'll be here in five minutes. Better get moving."

"Can't I stay home for one more day?"

Her mom smiled. "You've already missed five days of school. It will be good for you to get back with your friends and put this behind you."

Tabitha grabbed her schoolbag and jacket. The only good thing about getting stranded on a mountain with no food was that she hadn't thought about Melissa for days.

As she climbed aboard the bus, Cedar's words ran through her mind. *If you don't let them bother you, they stop.* She found an empty seat near the front, where the little kids sat, and rode to school in silence.

Her teacher smiled and said, "Welcome back," as she took her seat. Several students whispered behind their hands as she sat. Nothing had changed.

On the playground at recess, Melissa led a group of girls to her. "You been hiding from us?"

"No."

"So where were you?"

Why did she care? "Hiking." She looked away, across the field.

"You? Hiking?" Melissa snickered. "Oh, were you with those freakshow hippies who got caught on the mountain?"

Something inside Tabitha snapped. Who did Melissa think she was? As if she'd be able to survive what Tabitha had. She probably would have panicked and been swept down the river.

Tabitha spun to face Melissa, feeling strong, like a mother bear defending her cubs. "Those were my cousins. And, for your information, Ashley almost died this weekend." She took a step toward Melissa.

Melissa shrank back, looking for support behind her. The other girls stepped away.

Tabitha wanted to hit Melissa. To shake her until all of her snarky comments fell to the ground. But Cedar's face popped into her mind. That wouldn't get her anywhere. Melissa wasn't worth it anyway.

"You don't know anything." She turned and walked away, not checking once over her shoulder to see Melissa's reaction.

The rest of the day drifted by in a haze. She sped through her math problems and stared out the window, thinking about Max. Social studies was a blur. She was supposed to be reading about Aboriginal forms of travel, but the words wouldn't make sentences for her. Then her eye caught a picture of a canoe and her heart jolted. That was it. The canoe.

"May I go to the bathroom?" she asked.

Her teacher nodded.

She scooted past the bathroom and stood in the alcove by the water fountain. Peeking around the corner to make sure no teachers saw her, she pulled out her cell phone and dialed her cousins' house.

Cedar answered.

"How are they?" she asked.

"Doing better. Mom's arm is mostly healed. Ashley's able to move her jaw a bit. I might sleep tonight." He sounded exhausted.

"Who's going to get the canoe?"

He groaned. "I dunno. Me and Mom, I guess."

"How about you and me?"

Cedar paused. "Why? You hated it up there."

"I saw Max from the helicopter."

"Max is gone."

Tabitha shook her head, then realized that he couldn't see her. "I'm not talking crazy. I'm sure I saw him."

"You sure you want to go all the way back up there? The bear'll still be there."

Tabitha swallowed. What made her think she could face the bear? But they'd only be going for the day. Hike up. Pack the stuff. Find Max. Come home. "I can do it. I'm not like I was at the beginning of the trip."

"Don't you have to go to school?"

"Don't you?"

He sighed. "We'll go as soon as Ashley's out of the hospital. Mom won't want us to do this. We'll have to skip out. You up for that?"

Tabitha checked over her shoulder. Someone was walking down the hallway toward her. "Count me in. Call me. Got to go." She ended the call and half-ran back to her class.

Corinne stopped her in the hallway. She was one of the girls on the sidelines of Melissa's group. Not an active bully, but close enough.

"Teacher sent me to find you. Are you okay?"

Tabitha shrugged. "Yeah." She started to walk toward the room.

Corinne put a hand on her shoulder. "Wait."

Tabitha stopped and turned.

"My mom told me what happened at Lake Lovely Water."

Tabitha had a vague memory that Corinne's mom was a rock climber.

"She knew your uncle."

Tabitha nodded.

"It must have been hard up there," Corinne said.

Tabitha nodded once. "Sometimes."

"If you ever want to go hiking again, there's a group of us that go out every weekend."

Tabitha's mouth opened a crack. She managed a small nod as Corinne entered the classroom, then followed her without a word.

◎

On Sunday, Tabitha received the call from Cedar. "Tomorrow," he whispered. "Get the Greyhound bus from downtown. I'll pick you up at the Squamish terminal. Bring a backpack with space for the sleeping bags."

"Right."

"One more thing," Cedar said. "We're hiking to the ridge."

"What?"

"I'm bringing my dad's ashes."

"Are you crazy?" Tabitha said.

"I need to do this. Mom and Ashley will understand. They need to move on."

Tabitha hung up the phone. Everyone did need to move on, and by the time Ashley and Tess were strong enough to hike again, it would be too late to hike to the ridge. If Cedar didn't do it, they would have to wait another year.

But Tess and Ashley wouldn't understand. They'd be furious. Ashley would hate them forever for scattering

Bruce's ashes. Tabitha could live with Ashley's wrath, but was it worth it for Cedar to lose his sister's trust?

She put her hiking boots inside her backpack, along with extra clothes, water and food, and hid everything in a bush outside her house. Sleep took a long time to come as she lay worrying about lying to her parents, worrying about getting caught, worrying about going back up that mountain, worrying about the ashes, and most of all, worrying about Max. It had been five days since she'd seen him, eight days since she'd lost him. Even if he was still up there, would he have survived?

She did her best to appear normal at breakfast. Ate her cereal in silence. Watched her parents read their magazines. Rinsed her bowl. Had a moment of panic when her mom offered her a ride to school.

"No thanks, I'm walking with a friend."

Her mom smiled. "That's great!"

Tabitha cringed and lifted her schoolbag off the floor. "I'm going over to a friend's after school today. I'll be home late."

Big smile from her mom again. "Whose house?"

"Corinne's."

"Have fun. Call me when you need a ride home."

"See you." She ran out the door, chased by guilty feelings. She wasn't built for lying to her parents.

Checking to make sure no one was looking out the window, she pulled her backpack out of the bush and replaced it with her schoolbag.

She walked her usual route to school until she reached Cambie Street, where she turned right instead of left. Praying that no one would recognize her, she made a quick detour into the nearby grocery store for an important purchase, then jogged the two blocks to the SkyTrain stop and ran down the stairs.

She checked over her shoulder and pulled the change from her pocket with a shaking hand. Anyone watching would think she was doing something illegal. Then again, maybe she was. If playing hooky and lying to your parents was illegal.

She'd never taken the SkyTrain by herself. Her parents had taken her on it once to see a movie downtown. It was full of commuters heading to work. Tabitha might as well have had a sign that said *I'm skipping school* plastered to her head.

She had a plan though. If anyone asked her, she'd say she was going to an orthodontist appointment and hope they didn't want to know where it was.

The northbound train pulled into the station. Tabitha slouched in her seat, cradling her pack in her arms. Her heart was beating almost as fast as it had when the bear had taken their food. She'd never played hooky before. Never lied to her parents before. Not about something big like this. She took a deep breath to calm herself. All of this was for Max. Cedar might not believe her, but at least he'd agreed to let her come.

The train slowed and reached Pacific Centre station. She got off and stood for a moment, letting the commuters flow around her as she tried to get her bearings. A man dressed in a bright green fleece with a question mark on it began walking toward her. She froze. Was he coming to bust her and take her back to school?

"Need some help?" he asked. Under the question mark it said *SkyTrain Volunteer*.

"Um, yeah. I need to get to the Fairmont Hotel. Um, to see my orthodontist."

His eyebrows wrinkled, but he pointed up the stairs to Tabitha's left. "Take those up to Georgia Street and turn left. The hotel is two blocks away."

"Thanks." Tabitha sped away before he could ask any questions. As she climbed the stairs, she checked her watch. Twenty minutes until the bus arrived.

After walking a casual lap through the lobby of the hotel, pretending to be a tourist, she had to give in and ask the guy standing by the front doors.

"Excuse me, could you please tell me where the bus to Squamish picks up?"

He nodded. "Across the street. Flag it down."

"Thanks." She started heading for the corner to cross the busy road.

"Hey," he called.

Tabitha turned.

"Aren't you kind of young to travel by yourself?"

"Uh," she stalled. Her cheeks grew hot. "I'm going to visit my cousins. They'll be picking me up at the bus terminal." At least that was true.

"Oh." He didn't look satisfied with her answer. Tabitha didn't give him time to ask more questions. She crossed the road. Once she was on the other side of six lanes of traffic, he couldn't do anything.

The bus arrived a few minutes later. She waved to it, climbed on board, paid the driver ten dollars and found an empty seat.

Cedar was waiting for her at the Squamish station, an old canoe lashed to the top of Tess's beat-up Volkswagen van. Tabitha threw her pack in the back and hopped into the passenger seat.

"I feel like an escaped convict," she said. "Let's get out of here before people start asking questions."

Cedar lurched down the street.

"Are you allowed to drive?" Tabitha asked. She realized he'd never talked about driving before.

"I've got my learner's license. I'm allowed to drive, but only with a licensed driver in the car."

"Oh." Tabitha buckled her seat belt and slunk lower in her seat.

"As long as we don't get pulled over, we're fine. We'll be on the dirt road soon anyway," Cedar said.

Tabitha squeezed the door handle and closed her eyes. She wished hard for all the cops to be busy somewhere else.

"Did you tell your parents where we're going?" Cedar asked.

"Of course not! They'd never let me go back up there, especially without an adult."

He nodded. "I left Mom a note where she'd find it after we're already on the way."

Tabitha groaned. "Why'd you do that? She's going to call my parents for sure."

"I know. But we needed to let someone know where we're going. In case something happens and they need to come look for us."

Tabitha slumped in her seat. How could she have been so stupid? Here she was, ready to race up the mountain without telling anybody. Barely out of the house, and she'd already broken the first rule of hiking. At least she'd remembered food, clothes and water. "Did you bring a first-aid kit?"

"Yep. And extra chocolate."

Tabitha grinned. Of course he'd brought extra food. "How's Ashley?"

"Way better. Still tired. She won't be going back to school for a while."

"Lucky her."

"She *wants* to get back to school. Mom won't leave her alone. I think she feels guilty for what happened."

"It wasn't her fault."

"I know. But Ashley almost died."

"Does Ashley still think I'm the enemy?"

Cedar shook his head. "She's not talking crazy anymore. But she's sad about Max." He turned off the highway and onto the dirt road that would lead them to the river. Tabitha relaxed her hold on the door handle. At least they didn't have to worry about cops anymore. The van bumped down the road, making conversation impossible.

Tabitha watched out the window as they drove past fireweed and long grasses. She thought about Ashley. Her cousin would always blame her for losing Max. And maybe that was okay. If Tabitha's dad died, she'd want someone to blame too. It wasn't fair, but at least she knew why Ashley was doing it. If she and Cedar scattered Bruce's ashes, Ashley would really hate her, but at least it would be for a good reason.

And Ashley would always see her as the "younger" cousin—the one who'd never be able to do anything right. That wasn't fair either, but at least Tabitha knew it wasn't true. She'd survived on the mountain.

Survived and was ready to go back up, no matter what might be waiting for them up there.

Cedar parked the car in the small pull-out by the river, and they both climbed out. The river had receded to normal levels, although the water was a muddier brown than the first time they'd crossed.

CHAPTER EIGHTEEN

A knot started to form in Tabitha's stomach, but she willed it away and helped Cedar lift the canoe off the roof. As they carried it to the water's edge, she thought about that first day at Lake Lovely Water, when Cedar had seemed so big, loud and scary. It wasn't that he'd gotten any shorter, but he didn't seem to take up as much space as he had at the start of their trip.

They threw their packs into the canoe and clipped on their life jackets.

"Ready?" Cedar asked.

Tabitha nodded and stepped into the front seat.

Cedar pushed the boat from shore. "You paddle on one side, and I'll steer."

Tabitha panicked for a moment as the water caught the canoe. She closed her eyes and breathed deeply. She could do this. No sitting in the middle of the canoe feeling useless this time. She pulled her paddle through the water and felt the canoe move faster. Amazed, she pulled again.

"You got it," Cedar said.

In a few minutes they reached the other side and dragged the boat up the bank, over a fallen tree that had washed up during the flood. They tied it up to a stump, making sure it was well up the trail, away from the water, and shouldered their packs.

The trail climbed steeply away from them and was lost to sight within several meters. Everything was covered in a layer of mud and debris.

Tabitha sighed. She knew she could make it to the hut. She'd done it twice already. But her whole body felt tired at the thought of having to do it again.

"You sure you want to go through with this?" Cedar asked. "I can go myself. You can wait for me here."

Tabitha shook her head. "No way I'd let you go up there alone. That would be stupid." She pictured the yellow flash she'd seen from the helicopter. "I'll be fine."

"Let's see if we can find the other canoe. It's worth a lot more than our sleeping bags."

They searched along the bank, trudging through layers of branches and thick silt, until they finally found the canoe under some huckleberry bushes. It was scratched, but otherwise in good shape.

"Time to get going," Cedar said. "We'll get it when we come back." Halfway up the trail, they stopped for a water break. Tabitha lay down with her head on her pack and stared at the treetops. Everything felt different from the first trip up the mountain. She knew where they were going. Her legs didn't ache. Her shoulders were used to the weight of the pack. There was something else too, but she couldn't quite place it.

She laughed out loud when she figured it out.

"What?" Cedar said.

"There aren't any mosquitoes."

"The frost killed them."

Tabitha stretched her arms and legs. It felt great to be alive. "Good for the frost." She lifted a pinecone from the forest floor. "Did you know that pinecones are an example of the Fibonacci sequence?"

"The what?"

"The Fibonacci sequence. You know. One, one, two, three, five, eight, thirteen. Didn't you study it in math?"

"Maybe. It sounds sort of familiar," Cedar said.

Tabitha held up the pinecone. "The spirals at the base of a pinecone always come in Fibonacci numbers."

She traced the spirals. "See, if you count them this way, there are eight." She reversed directions. "If you count this way, there are thirteen."

Cedar grinned. "You are so weird. But that's cool."

Their next stop was the lake. Tabitha realized she'd been holding her breath, expecting Max to come bounding across the beach to greet them. But the lake was still. Not even a ripple broke the surface.

Cedar turned up the path to the hut. Tabitha followed, her shoulders drooping. She'd been so sure they'd find Max. Had she come all this way for nothing? It had been eight days since she'd lost him. She'd been kidding herself. Of course he hadn't survived.

As they approached the hut, Tabitha's pace slowed. Her senses prickled, feeling the air for the bear, as if she had antennae that would perceive it in the bushes.

Something whined.

Tabitha stopped. "Cedar, something's up there."

"Probably a squirrel."

"That wasn't a squirrel. What if it's the bear?" Tabitha whispered.

They heard it again.

"Maybe it's a bear cub," Tabitha said.

Cedar stopped. "It sounds like a whimper. I think it's under the steps of the hut."

Suddenly, Tabitha knew what it was. Putting aside all thoughts of the bear, she pushed past Cedar and ran for the stairs. She threw her pack on the ground and crawled underneath. Curled in a ball, snuggled amongst the bushes, lay Max. A very dirty, skinny, but otherwise healthy-looking Max.

"Max!" Tabitha shouted. The dog pushed himself to all fours and climbed on top of her, pushing her to the ground. She laughed as he licked her face. "I knew I'd seen you!" She wrapped her arms around his belly. "You must be starving. You're so skinny."

Cedar hurried up behind her. "Max!" Tears wet his eyes. Max trampled over Tabitha in his rush to get to Cedar, and the two of them rolled on the ground in a joyful reunion.

After a few minutes Cedar sat up and furrowed his brows. "I didn't believe you, Tabitha. And now we don't have enough food for Max."

Tabitha grinned and reached for her pack. She pulled out the bag of dog food that she'd bought on the way to the bus. "I was thinking positively."

Max leaped for the bag and tried to grab it from her hands.

"Oh no you don't," Cedar said. "You'll get sick if you eat that all at once." He held Max back as Tabitha poured the pellets into a plastic container she'd brought. Max slurped them up in three seconds and came looking for more.

"You can have more later," Cedar said.

Tabitha stuffed the bag of dog food back in her pack. "Maybe we shouldn't go to the top now."

Cedar eyed Max. "He can make it to the ridge. This is our only chance. We'll grab all the stuff on the way back."

"Right. I guess we'd better go then."

They shouldered their packs and started up the trail. Tabitha marked off sites in her mind as they passed—the spot she'd lost Max, the place she'd seen the bear the first time. Soon, however, they were around the lake and beginning to climb into new territory. Max trotted beside them, no worse for wear after more than a week on his own. Tabitha wondered if the squirrel population at the lake had gone down.

Cedar climbed in silence. Tabitha imagined the weight of Bruce's ashes pulling at his pack. Was he feeling guilty about scattering them without Tess and Ashley? Should she stop him?

After about forty-five minutes, the trail flattened. Cedar stopped beside a large boulder.

"This is the spot."

Tabitha turned to look behind her. The view was stunning. Lake Lovely Water glistened below them, surrounded by mountain peaks mottled with cracked blue glaciers. Streaks of yellow and orange trees ran through the forests like rivers.

"My dad loved this view. Sometimes he'd hike up here before anyone else was awake, just to drink his tea and watch the sunrise." Cedar sat on the boulder, staring at the red peak of the hut. Tabitha crouched beside him, stroking Max's fur.

"Let's do this," Cedar said. He opened his pack and pulled out the box of ashes.

Tabitha stepped away to give him room. She couldn't believe he was really going to do it.

He held a finger in the air to check the breeze, then motioned her over with his head. "You should help."

"Me?"

Cedar nodded. "After what we've been through, Dad would have wanted you to be a part of it."

Tabitha swallowed and stepped forward. Cedar began to lift the lid off the box. Just before it opened, she grabbed his arm. "Stop!"

Cedar jerked back. "What's wrong?"

"You can't do this. It will kill your mom and Ashley. They'll never forgive you."

Cedar wrapped his fingers tightly around the lid. "We have to end this. We need to move on."

Tabitha gripped his arm. The sun gleamed on the peaks behind him. "You can still move on." She swept her free hand in a circle, gesturing to the lake and the peaks. "It's about your memories. Not the ashes."

Cedar didn't let go of the lid. He stared hard at Tabitha for a long minute. Max nuzzled his legs. Tabitha held her breath.

He nodded. "I guess you're right." He held the box to his chest and turned toward the lake. After a moment he closed his eyes. He mumbled under his breath. Tabitha thought she heard the word *goodbye*. She stepped back and crouched to hug Max.

Several minutes later, Cedar wiped his cheeks with his sleeve. He stood and put the box in his pack.

Tabitha stepped forward and squeezed his hand. "Let's go home."

Cedar parked the van in front of his house. Tabitha noticed her parents' car parked in the driveway. She was going to be in so much trouble, she didn't even want to think about it. But right now they had something more important to do.

Ashley opened the front door and ran out to meet them.

"This better be good, Cedar," she said. "Everybody's freaking in there."

Tabitha smiled and opened the van door. Max bounded out to greet Ashley, almost knocking her down. For once, her cousin was speechless. She stared from Max to Tabitha, to Cedar and back again, as Max licked and pawed her.

"How…What?" she stammered.

Cedar grinned. "Looks like you owe Tabitha an apology. She found him. Knew he was there all along."

Tabitha held her breath, waiting for Ashley to lose it, to say that she was the one who hadn't wanted to leave.

But Ashley stayed quiet. After a moment she looked Tabitha straight in the eye and smiled. "Thanks."

Tabitha nodded. Good enough.

ACKNOWLEDGMENTS

While the characters in this book are fictional, some of the events are based on the experiences of Jane Millen and her family on their hiking trip to Lake Lovely Water in the 1980s. I am indebted to Jane, my friend and hiking partner, for sharing her story with me and allowing me to change it to suit my purposes. I have taken some liberties with the setting, keeping some details as they would have been thirty years ago (there is a tram across the river now) and modernizing others (no cell phones in the eighties). All mistakes are mine.

Many people helped bring this book to fruition. Thanks to: Nona Rowat for sharing *Family Stories,* her book of memories about the trip; Merilyn Simonds, writer-in-residence extraordinaire, for invaluable feedback; Paulette Bourgeois and Laisha Ronsau for help with early drafts of the story; my editor Sarah Harvey for her eagle eye. Thanks also to Stella Harvey, Sue Oakey, Nancy Routley, Libby McKeever, Katherine Fawcett, Mary MacDonald, Rebecca Wood-Barrett, Lisa Richardson and Pam Barnsley of the Vicious Circle, without whom this story would be sitting in a drawer.

Many thanks to the staff, students and parents at Spring Creek Community School for their interest in and support of my writing.

And a huge hug to my family, for their faith in me, their unfailing support and their love.

SARA LEACH is a writer and teacher-librarian in Whistler, British Columbia. She loves hiking the nearby alpine trails with her husband and two children. Fortunately, they have never been stranded in any mountain huts, although they have endured many rainy days. Sara's first book for Orca was *Jake Reynolds: Chicken or Eagle?* To learn more about Sara, please visit saraleach.com.